BLACKPINES
THE ANTLERS WITCH
THE LIGHT IN HER DREAMS

ADDISON LANE

Blackpines: The Antlers Witch:
The Light in Her Dreams

Copyright © 2022 Addison Lane

Cover design by Addison Lane

Addison Lane
addisonlane.net

Printed in the United States of America

First Printing: September 2022

ISBN 979-8-8496058-5-2

DEDICATION

To my patr(e)on saints, Kay and Lauren.

And to my wife and editor, Angela.

CONTENT GUIDANCE

This story explores topics related to violence, mental illness, grief and trauma, abuse, parental death, and kidnapping that may be upsetting for some readers. Additionally, please be advised that sex, coarse language, and alcohol consumption are also depicted.

i. lucía

*(if your heart could hold me,
we wouldn't have to pick up these pieces)*

Lucía dreams of flowers: dusky purple sage and burnt California poppies; frail taffeta clarkia and fringe-heavy seaside daisies; clusters of coastal buckwheat and fat bulbs of owl's clover. Maya hides, crouched beneath the pastel sagebrush. Her hair spills out behind her, sneaking away from the bush and taking root with the wild rye. Her curls have been brushed into a downy black blanket, and Lucía sits beside her, running her palms over the tendrils.

"Te amo, Maya," she whispers, and Maya sighs sweetly—stretching her long legs. "Will you come out?" But Maya remains napping under the rye. Lucía sighs in turn, twisting bits of hair around her fingers, moving them through chords that become more elusive all the time. She thinks this is A Major—the chord her father taught her first, sitting on the living room three days after Christmas. His plane was held up in Nevada for two hours—major delays across the country—and he'd missed Christmas Day.

She cups his cheek, smiling. He looks dashing in his pilot's uniform. He tips his hat, and a soft, huffing laugh—reserved (always) for him—fills her chest.

"Do you miss me, Papa?"

His hand covers her knuckles, and she feels the dream grow thin. She looks up, searching for its edges. Sometimes, in these lonely moments, she finds herself nearing her own dream's end, close enough to seize consciousness...

She rubs her eyes. Her father is gone, and Bruno is climbing the parade barrier.

"You're going to get in trouble."

He straddles it, feeling for the base with his toes.

"Bruno!"

Frustrated, she hooks her foot between the bars and climbs after her brother. His leg isn't long enough to reach the lower bar, and the gate rocks precariously as she struggles to get to the other side and help her brainy, clumsy little brother before he breaks his face open.

But the gate topples under their combined weight, and she squeals as the pavement rockets towards them. Adults are yelling around them. Abuela shouts over the din. They are in so much trouble. She lifts her head, blinking back stars. Blood streams from her chin—weightless and bright. She tries to catch it, but it circles her fingers, turns briefly into rings, and disappears.

How many little scars did she earn, taking care of Bruno and Jimena? Her chin, her lip, her arms, and her knees are testament to a lifetime of worrying—of throwing herself headlong into trouble to try to make their way a little easier. She rubs the scar on her chin, tongue poking through the broken part of her front tooth.

Nova said Maya is looking for her. She has suspected it. Maya is stupid the same way she is—stupider than anyone else she knows. Perhaps, she thinks, that's why she loves Maya so much. There is no one else—not even Abuela or Bruno or Papa—no one else she can trust so implicitly. If Maya is looking for her, Maya will eventually find her. Maya will wake her, and she'll finally be free.

The Witch passes through her dream, sharp-edged and hungry. She is looking for Nova, Lucía thinks, but Lucía has not seen him since that moment in the clouds. It's impossible to tell the time, but it feels like a lot has passed since then. He must have gotten away, and she feels glad and a little sad. It was nice to have someone to commiserate with. It was nice to feel real again.

The Witch stands over her, a monolith of black fabric and jagged white points. She casts a shadow over the dream, peering, speculating—her bloodless toes poking through the soft grass, and Lucía shrinks away from her, stinging all over. The Witch turns her face to the sky, and Lucía can see the white plane of her throat before she passes on and out of Lucía's dream, casting her net ever further—searching, searching, searching...

Lucía once again feels for the edge of sleep, wishing she could wake up for just a few minutes. She tries to let those feelings seep out of her, imagines them coming to the top of her skin like sweat and staining the forest around her so that Maya will know she has been here—so that Maya will not stop looking.

"Te amo, Maya. Te amo."

She wants to cry, but crying is no good in sleep. It doesn't release tension and frustration like it does in waking life. No, it makes everything so much worse.

Still, a sniffle escapes her, and she clutches her arms, looking up. Clouds roll overhead. They start out a grim bruise-green, but quickly thicken, and the sky flattens into an oppressive coal. She crouches, head between her knees, suddenly breathless. She tries to suck down air, but it's too thin in her lungs. The storm has stolen all the oxygen from her garden, and she is going to asphyxiate. Thunder booms, echoing in her bones, and she squeezes her eyes shut, trying to focus on breathing.

But the storm will not be ignored. The wind begins to whistle, and she shivers as dense gusts tear at her hair and neck, buffeting the garden and ripping flowers from stalks and limbs. Petals scream on the air, beating against her arms and back, and she presses herself to the earth, curling into a tight ball.

A great obelisk breaks through the dirt, bouncing her in place. It soars towards the storm clouds—lightning spilling over its tip, forming the pale branches of antlers. Another stabs upwards to her right. Another and another, until she is caged in. They circle her, close in on her.

They will devour her.

She looks up and sees the moon glowing behind the clouds.

"Help me! *Help me!*" she shrieks, grabbing her hair in both hands and sobbing dryly.

Time is running out. If Maya doesn't find her—

Tears bead on her lashes, one followed by another. They

trickle down her nose into the earth.

Maya won't let me down. Maya won't let me down. Maya won't let me down.

She thinks of Maya—the way her cheeks collect into plump, impish circles when she laughs, and how she sighs when she's just read something she really likes; the way she sticks her tongue out just a little when she's tired of hearing something; and the scent of her rich brown hands, wafting rose and chamomile. Her heart beats hard and solid in her chest, grounding her. Her love for Maya hurts and heals all at once, and the obelisks crumble, breaking into sand and blowing away with the last gusts of storm wind. She keeps her eyes closed, still listening for Maya's voice echoing from the shower, feeling for her cold toes nestled into the back of her knees.

Maya, *her* Maya...

The clouds break, and the tortured vines sigh in relief, revealing fresh flowers. Lucía lets their soft, baby petals cushion and cradle her, feeling worn and battered.

"Te amo, Maya," she whispers, a prayer, an adulation, an unheard *thank you*.

She sits, gently untangling buds of wildrose from her hair. It's quiet now. Too quiet. There is someone else in the dream, and it doesn't feel like the Witch.

Warily, she gets to her feet. Someone is watching her. Someone is following her. She swiftly turns the other way.

"Who's there?!"

But they're already gone.

ii. harper

*(they learned early,
all it took was a wooden horse to get into your heart
and burn it down)*

He's always found stumbling into someone else's dreamscape awkward, but it happens all the time, and coming out of the wrong dream is hardly surprising at the Libra Lodge—or "the L," as Libra lovingly refers to it. He hasn't stayed here since he was 11, but it hasn't changed much. The rooms still remind him of gated Poconos communities—the cabin walls artfully mismatched and purposefully distressed; rustic couches piled with old quilts; a stupidly long dinner table with a small army of random chairs; and an enormous fireplace perpendicular to an empty bar. The smell is also unpleasantly nostalgic. It reminds him of his parents and better times, and then of everything that's happened in the past 48 hours.

He rubs his eyes, grinding sleep's crust into their corners, then curses softly, trying to dab them clean. But the damage is done: they sting. His neck aches from leaning over the bed, and he slowly rises, gingerly stretching.

Out of a stranger's nightmare and into his own. But yesterday was worse. For the first time, he'd come awake with the pull of Hirst's pack in his gut. Mason missed all the puking, and he's glad about that. He seems like someone who'd give Harper a hard time about violent illness, no matter how temporary, and Abbott's sad, worried stare was enough coddling.

He can feel the pack again this morning. He will feel them, he thinks, for the rest of his life, unless he finds some way to break that spell.

Break the spell?

He cups the back of his neck, cringing, and stands.

He *could* try breaking the spell. If it's magic that makes an alpha, maybe murder isn't the only way to free himself, and breaking the spell could be easier than trying to kill Hirst. He hates himself a little for considering anything but vengeance, but he has faced Hirst twice now, and both times...

He feels nauseated again and sits hard on the corner of the bed. Nova doesn't stir. Oren's grandmother, Ambrosia, spent most of the morning fussing over him with her assistant and protégé, Lila. He supposes even if they don't know how to handle secrets and sensitive situations, the Libra elders know how to patch up bites and scratches. They've assured him that Nova's more bruised than broken, no matter how sorry and small he looks under his pile of quilts and blankets.

Harper hasn't been able to look Mason in the eye since the morning after the full moon. It isn't his fault: he told Mason to stay away for exactly this reason, and the dumbass is lucky he wasn't eviscerated. But still, there's a part of Harper that feels responsible. Those people are not his pack, but also they are, and now maybe Mason is stuck in the same shit situation he's in. He doesn't even know how to broach the subject with a *new* wolf, not when he's still trying to come to terms with what it means for his own little world.

He leans over his knees, forehead in his palms. "Fuck."

Maya hates him. Mason probably hates all of them. And Nova—

He sighs and drops his hands. The little bastard seems pretty comfortable right now, a wild tangle of hair spilling over the top of his pillow, the rest of him hidden under Blanket Mountain. He looks wan, though—pale beneath his normally golden brown skin. Harper takes a breath, holds it, and puts the back of his hand to Nova's temple. He's warm for someone that washed out. He's also curled so tight, it takes Harper a moment to realize he's shivering. Harper considers curling up behind him except it would feel too real in their human bodies. He looks down at his hand, warm from Nova's skin.

He wishes he was better at this.

He moves closer, until he's leaning into the curve of Nova's stomach, resting against his knobby knees. The Nova under these covers is different from the clueless kid Maya dragged home. His skin is full of galaxies and ghosts, covered in scribbles that Harper only recognizes from social media. He wonders how Nova, living out of his car and existing hand to mouth, managed to pay for all that ink. A friend, maybe? But those stupid hazel eyes are so hard to say 'no' to, so maybe a favor. He smiles a little.

And then he frowns.

He can only guess Hirst nabbing Nova has something to do with Maya. If Nova remains in Jersey, Hirst might come for him again. Worse, he might make Harper bring Nova to him. He shudders, remembering the intensity of that order—how close he came to attacking Nova. His stomach complains, sending sour envoys up his throat in warning. They should get Nova back to L.A. as soon as possible.

But then, Nova must have been in L.A. when they found him.

An uneasy feeling ripples down his spine. If Hirst wants Nova back, how far will he have to run to get away?

Just then, his stomach surges, and Harper manages to grab the waste bin before what's left of yesterday's dinner returns.

"Fugggh," he grunts, trying not to breathe in, and he hurries outside to find a faucet.

Padding down the hallway, bin at his side, he tries not to attract attention, but it finds him anyway. The bathroom door cracks, and Oren appears, peeking in.

His nose wrinkles, but he's kind enough to ask, "You okay?"

"Mrr," Harper replies, trying to sound gruff and unapproachable, but Oren trails after him, into the showers, as he rinses out the can. He stands just out of sight, fidgeting, because Oren is always fidgeting: scraping his thumb along the side of his hand, sucking his lips between his teeth, or kicking under the table...

"How's your friend?" Oren abruptly asks, and Harper sighs.

"Asleep."

"Oh, I meant— I saw the other one go out earlier. He was playing fetch with the dog."

Harper considers. Maybe Mason is taking things better than expected. He *did* seem to be pretty into the whole wolves and witches and vampires thing (though Harper is pretty sure vampires really are imaginary).

Or maybe he's just trying to think of anything except what's happened.

"Maybe you should—"

"Talk to him? Maybe *you* should talk to him."

"I don't know him."

"Neither do I."

Oren is silent, but not cowed. Cowed Oren is different from Quiet Oren. Cowed Oren bows his head over his sandwich while Caleb Greer makes fun of his belly. He doesn't say anything when the other boys are too rough with their pushing and shoving. He feigns deafness when the white kids repeat their parents' fucked up jokes. He smiles thinly and waits for the bad to be over with a miserable patience that has always infuriated Harper.

Harper, spiteful and hardened, had often wanted to hurt the people who attacked Oren's gentleness, who tried to make him feel small for still believing that the world isn't a complete dumpster fire—who never realized they were experiencing someone beautiful and rare. But maybe that's why he didn't say anything back then either, because making sense of Oren is hard for Harper, too, and probably, if he's being honest, Oren's kindness scares him.

Still, knowing that someone like Oren exists has always

been a secret relief. Throughout their high school years, Harper had lived in fear that that light would go out, and the world would prove itself to be as dark as he suspected it truly was.

Or maybe he just has always hated Caleb Greer and Angus Walsh, and hating them on Oren's behalf—hitting them on "Oren's behalf"—was a good excuse for a lot of things.

Speaking of...

"Are the fucktwins here?" he asks, leaving the bin upturned over the drain and going to rinse his mouth.

"No, they left after breakfast. They were the only ones who were hungry, but I guess that's good. It would suck if Lila's cooking went to waste."

Harper swallows back a slew of observations regarding the sociopathy of certain wolves and rubs his mouth on the hem of his shirt.

"The thing is," Oren persists, "I think that the only person here who knows what he's gone through is you."

Harper realizes they're both staring at his scar, and he immediately turns red, furious that he doesn't have something to cover it with. He puts his hand over it, fingers puckering the muscle. Oren says nothing, watching him with the kind of clemency that makes it hard for Harper to lash out. He stares into his own blue eyes and glares. Because that's what it is: he's the one he hates most right now.

"I was so fucking useless," he says quietly, accusation in his voice, aimed straight at his reflection.

Oren remains silent, and Harper is grateful for his understanding.

He closes his eyes and sighs, ducking his head so he doesn't have to look at himself anymore. He turns to face Oren, still in full glower, and Oren remains unflinching. Harper thinks he used to be much more intimidating. He supposes he's just a sorry loner these days. He's been defanged by the world of adulthood.

Or maybe it's because he was pathetic enough to have admitted failure at all. Shame burns a hot trail through his chest, and he looks away, but Oren just puts a broad hand on his wrist.

"It's cool, man," he says. "Sometimes— I don't know. Only, I know it isn't your fault."

Something inside him wavers, and Harper almost admits it—

I can feel him inside me. I can feel him in my head.

But that would be absolute proof that all of this is true, and he's not that brave.

More gently than usual, he pulls away from Oren's touch, nodding tightly.

"There you are."

Manu pokes his head through the door, hair tumbling over his shoulder, looking much too clean and shiny for a night spent fighting evil wolves. He smiles, glancing between Oren and Harper with some apprehension (at least Harper's still intimidating to *someone*; he wouldn't want to forfeit all his boundaries in the space of 72 hours).

"We're going to play some pool. There's beer."

"You coming?" Oren asks.

Harper glances down the hall, his eyes drawn towards Nova's room.

"Lila said she'd be back to check on him by two. Besides," Manu says, one hand splayed on the frame, leaning back to look over his shoulder, "I think he has company right now. He'll be okay."

"Yeah, sure. You got anything stronger than beer?"

Oren puts a hand on his shoulder and laughs. "We've known where Grams keeps the bar keys for *years*."

"It's why Caleb had to be nice to us," Manu adds.

"That was 'nice'?"

Oren laughs again, and it's a happy, rich sound that makes Harper hurt and relax all at once. There's a strange feeling in his chest, like he's missed out on something. This could have been his pack. But instead—

"That's a face," Manu says, shaking his head. "Come on. We've got the cure for all your ills."

∘ ∘ ∘

"Was that Maya last night?" Mayhem asks, lining up her shot. Manu reaches out with his toe, poking her. "Cut it out," she says and then she giggles and looks at him over her shoulder with *that* kind of expression. Harper runs his hand up his face, wondering how buzzed he is.

"Are you two...?" he asks, deciding that being on the edge of drunk means he doesn't have to pretend he isn't interested, or filter.

Manu grins shyly, and Mayhem smirks before nailing two balls. They clack and bounce off the sides before neatly disappearing into the table. She moves to the other side to put another in the pocket, wagging a finger. "I won him in a pool game."

Manu laughs, head ducking. "You're so rude."

She winks and returns her attention to the striped balls spread across the green felt. "So? Was that Maya?"

Harper grunts, turning to rub his cheek on his knuckles.

"I haven't seen her since middle school. When did *she* get wolfed?" Oren asks, peeling the label from his bottle.

The tipsy, easy part of Harper considers spilling, but he pushes his chin down on the tops of his hands and looks away, refusing to blurt out facts that don't belong to him. "High school, I guess."

"Are you on the outs? Why didn't she stick around?" Mayhem asks, finally failing to sink her ball, and Manu steps up to the table, rubbing his chin.

"Don't act like you don't know."

She lifts an eyebrow. "I *don't* know."

Harper bites his tongue, tries again. "There have been developments. Bad ones."

"What do you mean?" she asks, watching the muscle flattening over the bones in Manu's forearm. It's a nice view.

The cue wobbles beneath him, and Harper jerks, frowning at his insolent perch. He considers the wisdom of keeping it to himself, but decides if he's drunk enough that he needs the cue to stay upright, he might as well do away with reservation.

"Do you know anything about magic?"

"Not really. Lupe might, and Ms. Ambrosia and Lila do." She glances at him, canny and unpleasant. He does his best to avoid her gaze. "I thought your aunt also dabbled."

"What kind of magic do you want to do that you don't

want to ask your aunt about it?" Manu asks, his shot a perfect set of motion that sends the balls beating the sides and each other and rolling to stops well beyond any hole.

"How much do you *actually* know about Maddox Hirst and my parents?"

Mayhem withdraws her scrutiny, frowning between Oren and Manu. They look between each other and shrug.

"What they told us, I guess," Manu says. "One night, Hirst went into your house and had a fight with your parents, and he just..."

"Lost it," Oren supplies.

Manu nods. "He killed them, and then he turned a bunch of people and ran off. No one saw him again—not until now."

"Do you know what they were fighting over?"

Manu shakes his head.

Harper frowns. "I don't either, but I feel like your elders do. They're hiding something, and I just...I feel like maybe if I knew why, things would finally make sense. Because that was the story I grew up with, too, and it never made sense to me, and it makes even less sense now, because my dad... He's not dead. He was there. He's the one who ran off first."

"Shit," Oren mumbles.

"Shit," Mayhem echoes.

"Fuck-fuck."

Manu looks around, shrugging. "I didn't want to get jinxed." He turns back to Harper, earnest once more. "What does that mean, though? Why is he...? I mean, that was Hirst's pack, right?"

"You *know* why," he replies, training his eyes on his toes.

"Shit," Mayhem repeats, so soft and so loud in the ensuing silence.

"Grams might know a spell," Oren finally says. The hope in his voice sounds strained, but Harper feels grateful anyway. "She's the best witch in Jersey, so she might have ideas at least. Ask her—you know, when she comes back to check on your friend."

"His boyfriend, you mean," Mayhem says, pointing at Harper with her cue.

"Wait, which one?" asks Manu.

"*Neither* one, and fuck you guys."

"Okay, so not boyfriend present tense, but Sleeping Beauty was definitely a boyfriend in a past tense capacity," Mayhem replies, leaning over the pool. "Or else you wouldn't be so mad right now."

"Whatever you say." He leaves his cue propped against the wall and goes to the mini fridge to procure another beer.

"So Harpy *is* fucking one of them."

Caleb Greer comes stomping down the basement stairs, Angus at his heels, and Lupe trailing behind them with grocery bags swinging from her arms.

"You guys could at least help me carry some of this," she huffs, dumping the bags on a nearby table. "You know, instead of starting fights with Harper?"

"Easy, Harpy. I mean no harm." Caleb bats his eyes, lifting his hands in supplication.

Angus sighs, pushing past him to sift through the groceries, freeing a bag of chips for his personal consumption and dropping unceremoniously onto the couch.

"*Hey!*" Lupe scolds (and is ignored).

"Don't take everything so fucking seriously, Harper."
Caleb flops next to Angus, shoving a hand into the bag and
filling his mouth with chips. "Bad for your blood pressure."

Harper realizes he's clutching the beer bottle like he's
going to throw it at Caleb's dumb blonde head. He takes a
deep breath, counting backwards. Mayhem puts down her
cue and takes a step forward, but they aren't 15 anymore. He
isn't going to give Caleb Greer a black eye—or anything else.

Especially not anything else.

"Where's the bottle opener?" he asks, turning away from
Caleb.

Manu holds out a hand, popping the cap with his keys,
and the mood settles back into a lazier place.

"Here," Lupe says, taking the chips from Angus and
handing them to Harper. He accepts the bag with a stifled
sigh and goes to sit in an armchair across the room from the
intruders.

"Did they have..." he starts, feeling his face grow hot. "...
cotton candy?"

Lupe shakes her head, smoothing her bangs over her
brow. Her hair used to be long—the kind of long that
screamed, *I'm sad inside! Why can't you see me?* It's shorter
now—some kind of punk-slash-pixie fade. Less sad, more, *Say
that again, motherfucker.*

"It suits you," he says, and she begins patting the top of
her head, her cheeks growing red.

"No, they— Um, sorry. They didn't. Sorry."

"When did you start eating girl candy?" Caleb asks,
throwing a chip and missing horribly. Harper lets the shame
of Caleb's failure stand for a retort.

"He likes it," he tells the rest of the room. "Nova."

It's a name that feels like Pop Rocks on his tongue—bright and crackling; not painful, but not soothing either. It's the sound of a firecracker bursting into a million sparks and leaving only the memory of light against a smoky sky. It's the best and worst four-letter word in his vocabulary.

Mayhem shakes her head, offering a sympathetic look. Manu and Oren politely avert their eyes.

"What kind of name is 'Nova'?" Caleb demands through a mouthful of chips—a high school era move he liked to pull when he was feeling especially petulant. And Harper rolls his eyes, intent on denying Caleb an answer—his go-to for when equal and opposite petulance was the best reply.

"The kind you give your kid when you want him to be a rockstar."

Mason appears at the top of the stairs, his expression wavering between defiant and terrified. He rubs his elbow with increasing intensity, and Harper imagines any defiance is doomed to be short-lived in the face of Caleb's disregard.

"I thought moms never wanted their kids to be musicians," Caleb says, though with surprisingly less belligerence and a great deal more uncertainty than expected. He even swallows before he speaks.

"Amaris isn't a run-of-the-mill mom," Mason replies, going red beneath his freckles, but he braves the steps and descends a little further.

Harper does his best to stop looking at Mason, suddenly stiff and cramped despite all the beer and the expanse of his armchair.

"How's your shoulder?" Oren asks, wise beyond his years,

and Harper is more grateful for his existence than he has ever been. Truly, he has never appreciated Oren Fisher half enough. He wishes he'd understood that before. He vows to remedy this going forward.

Mason comes the rest of the way into the basement, his hand moving from his elbow to the bandage swelling under his grimy t-shirt. He stares at his toes, the color gone from his face. "It's...it's okay," he mumbles.

Harper throws back the rest of his beer—all of it, until it burns the back of his throat, bubbles in his guts like he'll be spewing it if he doesn't stop, but he gulps it down anyway, feeling himself slip from tipsy-drunk to drunk-drunk.

"'M check Nova," he says, setting the bottle beside his chair and floundering to his feet. He tosses the bag of chips back to Angus and weaves past Mason to the stairs. Mason opens his mouth to say something, but maybe neither of them are ready to say anything, because he closes it again and turns his attention to the wolves now offering him snacks and a place at the pool table.

Harper hurries up the stairs as fast as he can without falling on his face. But his steps slow and soften when he reaches the top floor landing, afraid that the weight of his boots might wake Nova, bring him back too suddenly to the world of sensation and pain. (Though he hopes— It would be nice, is all, if he was the one who happened to be there when Nova woke up.) He stops in the doorway, breathing shakily, and gazes at the bed.

Nova is still asleep.

Nova is still beautiful.

From that first moment...

Maya tossing her bags down the hall, smelling like unfamiliar forests and someone else's laundry detergent, and shouting his name with glee (and a trace of consternation) before ushering her hostage into the living room—

This is Nova.

Heart-faced, floppy-haired, hazel-eyed Nova, who smiled crookedly and bathed the room in starlight. It felt like the temperature had gone up 20 degrees. It was like walking outside after hours in the dark university library. Suddenly everything felt like *summer*—the kind of summer in books and movies, the kind that's endless hours of cloud watching and the smell of sun-baked honeysuckle and the mineral softness of creek water around your ankles...

The tip of Nova's nose was peeling from a recent sunburn. He was coltish in the arms and legs and square in the middle—and so very short. And all Harper could do was gape, his heart doing acrobatics he'd never felt before.

Nova tossed his hair, let it sway back and forth over his eyes in a gleaming, impossibly soft wave, and then he laughed this awful, squeaky elf laugh.

You look like you've seen a ghost, and you don't even know me yet!

Nova's hair is long past the point of shape, tangled with leaves and dirt and the knots that always find their way into wavy hair over time. Harper, fingers buzzing with beer, heart overexposed by trauma, begins to pick the easiest pieces out with his fingers.

What's the most interesting thing anyone's ever told you?

Nova's heels banged the cupboards as he cradled his coffee to his belly.

I don't know.

Whale sharks are filter-feeders. They're the largest fish on earth.

He turned his copper-green eyes on Harper and smiled until the skin around them crinkled. The morning light caught in his left eye, and it blazed, golden.

"Nova," Harper murmurs, his hand forgetting its task, coming to rest on Nova's jaw. He leans forward, and his hair falls over them—a dark brown canopy, a story that they used to tell that he'd half-forgotten...

A story that's over.

Harper leans back, ashamed. Nova sleeps on, comfortably pressed against his hand, like Harper is the sun and Nova just a flower.

"You melt my brain, starchild," he whispers, his throat constricting.

He does his very best to think about anything except how much he missed Nova. He quashes the need to gather Nova into his arms. This doesn't change anything. Nova still left him (years ago, at that), Mason's been bitten by Hirst, and Maya hates him. Aunt Jelly and Uncle Heath have been lying to him for years, and Harper is an active threat to everyone around him. Nothing has changed. Nothing is good. He isn't sure how it can get good, coming out of all of this. But his stomach interrupts his melancholy, roiling upwards and necessitating an immediate release.

He stumbles away from Nova and to the toilet, finding fresh solace in the cold porcelain ring.

iii. lucía

*(you're magma under the ocean,
you start off molten,
but life just leaves you cold)*

There are seven people at most—all of them here to see
Busted Lip once Backyard Ghosts clears the stage. Lucía
shouldn't be anxious. There aren't enough people to make
her feel bad about herself, even if they end up virulently
hating the band and throwing cans at the stage, but it's
Lucía's first show that isn't a school talent contest, or
an informal jam session at a house party. She rubs her
hands on her jeans, but her palms seem to have become
persistently clammy.

"Man, this is ass."

She glances at Datton, busy smoothing her hair across her
forehead, her short nose wrinkled and her lip drawn back
like when Brunilda says they have to go over a song *again.*
Lucía self-consciously pats her hair. It looks like she woke
up this way (because she did), but Datton always makes her
feel weirdly self-conscious. Datton's been part of the scene
since she was 13 and playing in bands since she was 15, and

Lucía wishes that was her story, but Papa taught her how to play guitar, and it was all Rolling Stones and some bluegrass licks *his* dad had taught him. Her parents were not about to let her go to punk shows at 13. That was just never going to happen.

She tries to recall the first show she was allowed to attend: four guys with customs and amps that cost more than her family's computer. They'd been self-conscious and swaggering all at once (probably drunk)—sagging skinny jeans and checkered sneakers, dyed hair and facial piercings. She wasn't *into* them, but her 14-year-old self hungered for the aesthetic.

They weren't even good, and she'd kept thinking to herself, *I could do this. I could do better.* All those girls surging against each other, crammed against the front of the stage—that could be *her* writhing audience. She could give them a *real* reason to get excited.

Why should boys have all the fun?

Seven people are not enough to form a writhing mass. They mostly look bored anyway, drinking beer from plastic cups and milling in a circle near the bar.

"It's not about numbers. Not yet," Brunilda says, rubbing her hands and cracking her neck. She drags her fingers through freshly pink hair and smiles, but it doesn't carry enough confidence to stabilize Lucía's heart, or to wipe the pout from Datton's mouth. Brunilda sighs. "Come on."

They file onto the stage, Datton sneering at the not-crowd as she settles behind her drum kit, but Lucía hangs back. Brunilda slides her guitar across her chest, and Harumi gathers her bass, but Lucía stands dumbly in place until

Harumi gives her a gentle nudge, and she remembers to slip the strap over her head. She desperately tries to recall how to play their songs. They only have five to get through.

Datton begins tapping a cymbal, and instead of introducing them, Brunilda screams. Seven heads, plus the bartender, snap to attention, and Lucía doesn't even breathe, she just lets the tap of Datton's drumsticks become the pattern of her heart, and she hits the first chord. Seven heads start bobbing, and her fingers cut across the strings on muscle memory alone.

Pink electricity snakes out from her fingertips, jumping from the guitar and sending rainbow-hued sparks floating to the ceiling. She leans her hand to the strings and feels the chunky, percussive roar of the palm mute rumble through the amps. It gnaws at her bones, shakes her blood in her veins like some kind of fantastic, terrible cocktail of sound and iron, and she is so desperately happy. She does her best to follow Datton's lead, to not outpace Harumi's bass or Brunilda's singing.

The club fills with flares of pink and gold, streamers of purple and bursts of green. It's a cloud of music, changing shape and hue with each new riff. Seven people become seventeen, become seventy, become seven hundred, and it's not a club, but a festival spreading out across late summer grass. The air thickens with the smell of beer and grease and the sterile note of new cotton.

She watches herself from behind a horde of bodies in black hoodies and cut off shirts—hair stained pink and green and blue, skin covered in permanent marker and song lyrics. She can hardly see herself over the crowd. She jumps and hoots, pumping her fist and bobbing her head in time with the other Lucía. On stage, her hair is short and jagged—sweaty and wild. Her jeans slip down her hips, kept in place by a pink studded belt (her lucky belt). She doesn't look at the crowd. She's lost in the music, looking up only to make eye contact with Harumi, or to straddle Brunilda's knee as their desperately strummed sections beat against each other and intertwine.

"Get on my shoulders!" Maya shouts, bending down enough for Lucía to hop onto her hips and get her thighs around Maya's waist.

"You're the best, My-Ya." She plants a kiss on the top of Maya's head and looks up.

But it's not her band anymore. It's boys with faux-hawks and chucks, playing songs about the high school girls who broke their hearts, and Lucía's excitement seeps out of her. She peers over the crowd, trying to find Backyard Ghosts, trying to remember that moment of elation, but they've already been forgotten—a flicker of light, outshone by newer and more popular acts.

"Are you looking for *her*?" Maya asks in a soft, venomous tone.

"What? No, I'm—"

How can she explain to Maya? How can she let her know that this isn't a zero-sum. She loves Maya, *and* she loves music.

"Then why couldn't you make time for me?"

And Maya disappears.

Lucía hits the ground, the earth sinking around her, and she is afraid that it will keep sagging, that she'll be dragged down to the molten, fatal center of the planet.

"Maya! *Maya!*"

A strange hand seizes her by the wrist, pulling her from the deflating balloon of grass. Her rescuer hauls her onto the empty stage—a single island at the heart of a vast grey nothing.

"Whoa," she gasps, skittering back from the edge.

"You afraid of heights?"

"I'm afraid of *voids.*"

Lucía turns to the stranger. He is, in most respects, unremarkable—an average middle-aged white man: thin-lipped, greying, and tired. She smiles gingerly and extricates herself from his grip, walking backwards to the drum kit and sitting down. Ash drifts from the sky—burned out ticket stubs and band stickers, a poster of Mice in Love (*That's my band now; that's my real band*, she thinks), and shredded setlists. Cinders settle on her knees, and she blows them away, shaking them from her hair.

"This dream sucks."

The man laughs. It only makes him sound exhausted. He comes to sit beside her, catching soot in his hands and pressing it into a ball.

"You're too old for snowball fights," she huffs, wrapping her arms around her knees and settling her chin in the groove.

"I used to have a great arm, though," the stranger replies, tossing the ball into the air. It falls apart, sending glittering ash across the stage. "Snow is easier to work with."

"Who are you?"

"Well, I'm hoping you'll see me as an ally."

She turns, leaning on her cheek, and frowns at him. "That's the kind of thing people say when they want something from you."

"Fair enough. But I imagine there are things you might want from me, too."

"Hmm... What *do* you want from me?"

"I want to know where you are—where the Antlers Witch is."

Lucía laughs, shaking her head. "I'd like to know that, too. But since you're here, you must be close. What do you want with her?"

"I'm guessing she hasn't told you much about herself."

Lucía pauses, but shakes her head.

"We call her a witch, but she's more than that. Not quite a god, but not one of us either. It's difficult to fathom her power."

"But I'm guessing you can. And what? You think you can take that from her? Good luck. I don't think it'll be like sneaking gum from the checkout line."

He lifts his face, and the ash collects in his mouse-grey brows, on his bleached out lashes and chalky skin. His face is quiet, composed—terrible.

"It is possible. When she moves from one body to the next, she's vulnerable. If you take advantage of that moment of weakness, you could take her power and leave her soul. Do you understand? You'd have all her power and none of the danger of her soul swallowing yours."

The hairs on the back of her neck jump to life. She straightens, swallowing thickly, and shifts away from him. "You're making it sound very simple, but I don't think—

Have you really thought this through? Do you really wanna take that risk? If you lose, she'll gobble you right up."

He shakes his head. "Perhaps it is a risk, but I *have* thought about it, and I'm willing to take it. There are times in life when you don't have a choice—you have to go all in. It doesn't matter that you might lose. What matters is that you could win."

Her throat feels thick, coated in smoke, in fear, in disturbed realization. She remains very still, afraid that if she moves too quickly, he'll hear the frightened treble of her heart and know that she knows.

"You don't want to disappear, right?" he continues. "I want her power, and I have the knowledge, the skill, and the resources to take it. If we trade places, we both win."

She eyes the edge of the stage. "You're probably not the first to try and pull a fast one on her. The odds are against you, and if she takes over your body, you'll fade until there's nothing left. I know that much. And there's no way around that. It's how— It's how she survives."

(*And what if you don't win or lose?*

What if you break her magic trying?)

She stares down at her hands, surprised to find them still. She squeezes her fingertips into her palms, stares at the tendons swelling against her skin, and exhales very slowly from between her teeth.

"Your concern is very kind. You're too kind of a person to disappear like this."

He studies her profile. Her eyes flick to him and away again. It feels like he's looking at a Rubik's cube, searching for the move that'll slip everything into place. She glances at him once more and gives in, rubbing her arms. He smiles.

"She's an old thing, and we live in a young world. Don't you think there's a better way? It doesn't seem fair, taking someone like you prisoner and destroying them. The world needs *more* people like you, not less. If someone with a fresher outlook were to replace her... This world is full of sadness. It's full of tragedy and unfairness. She has lived, mired in all of that, for years and years. She has become immune to human sadness. Instead of using her power to better the world, she's made herself content to observe. But I'm tired of watching bad things happen."

"Are you the one—" She swallows thickly. "Did you kidnap Nova?"

He turns back to her, his gaze steady.

"Yes."

"Did you hurt him?"

He grows still, watching without blinking. "No," he says softly, earnestly. The lie is so perfectly executed she almost believes it.

She scratches at the tears in her jeans, trying to breathe around the lump in her throat. Carefully, she asks, "What will happen if she gets left behind? If you take her magic and shut the door on her soul? What happens to her?"

"Her chapter will end, as it should have ended long ago. She'll die, and we'll enter a new era, where life is kinder and better for everyone."

"You really believe that, huh?" Her voice trembles. She gets to her feet, wrapping her arms around herself, and shuffles towards the edge of the stage to peek over the side. It's no longer the grey of nightmares, but the black of a dream opening nearby. She clears her throat. "She didn't choose you, though. She won't take you just because you volunteer. She's too smart to— No, you just can't do it. And even if you could... I see. I see now."

"What is it?"

Her eyes narrow on the maw below her. "You took Nova, because you thought it'd get you closer to Maya—closer to *me*."

"We're running out of time. She's going to transition soon. *Lucía—*"

She flinches, gripping her elbows tighter.

"You'll be dead soon, and you won't be able to do anything about it. She's keeping you against your will—"

"But I don't think it's that simple," she whispers. "I think if you really were that smart, you'd realize it, too. If you try to kill her... No, you can't even try. Thanks for the talk—" She turns, looking at him over her shoulder. "—but stay away from us." She sucks in air, inhales hard enough to make her lungs hurt, and hurtles into the blackness.

"Lucía!" The stranger rushes to the edge of the stage, pausing, and then he, too, leaps.

"Fucking—"

She turns, arms and legs pressed tight as she dives through the darkness. Everything is so solidly black, she can't tell if she's falling fast, or if this has turned into a slow-motion parody of an escape scene. There's light ahead of her, though, and she opens her arms, giving herself great, dark wings, and swoops towards it. She plunges into the next dream, crashing into red rocks and purple twilight. The dream quivers beneath her, the moon-whitened sand rippling towards umber hills, uprooting sage and desert senna, and frightening pink lizards and starry scorpions. She scrambles to her feet, casting about. Maybe this dreamer is far away enough that the strange man can't follow.

Maybe.

But she can't risk it.

She sprints towards the dream's center, towards the golden glow of a campfire stretched towards the sky. Glimmering flakes of ash spiral upward, painting new constellations atop an oddly bright sky. A single figure stands before the bonfire: small, stocky, luminescent, and dangerously familiar. She puts her heels down, spraying white sand in her wake. Looking over her shoulder, she can see the stranger's shadow stretching alongside the pronged silhouettes of cacti. He will find them in seconds. She sprints forward, grabbing Nova's elbow and dragging him around to face her.

"Lucía?" He looks down at her hands, clenched in the skin above his elbow, and then up at her face, blinking owlishly. Her urgency should be a wildfire, sweeping him up and burning through him, but his face is buried in placid bemusement.

She gives him a shake. "Nova, you have to wake up. You have to wake up *right now.*"

"What do you mean?" he asks, red-orange chips erupting from the fire, dusting his hair and shoulders without singing. He glows softly—too new and strange for even this place. "Are you in danger?" He looks upwards to where the sparks meet the sky, and she can see that he has written something in the stars—half-formed gibberish.

"It's a poem," he tells her with some satisfaction. "It

explains every—"

She shakes her head and resumes shaking him. "Nova, wake up! Wake the fuck up!"

"I don't under—"

The stranger is crossing the desert with long, purposeful strides—too cocksure to run, but not taking his time either.

"Nova!" she screams, fisting his shirt and burying her brow in his throat. "He's going to kill us. We have to— You have to wake up. *Wake up, Nova!*"

"Who is that?" Nova asks, gently prying her away.

"A very bad person. You have to get out of here. Wake up already, you stupid—"

"No, I don't think it's a person. It has antlers."

Lucía whirls around, breath stuck in her throat. The Witch is unfolding from the star-shadows of the rocks: first her antlers, and then her shoulders, black and hunched as she drags herself across the distance of their bodies and into Nova's dreamscape. The stranger continues towards them, unaware of her—for now.

She turns back to him. "He can't see her. Please, Nova. *Please,*" she whispers, fingers tightening in his shirt. "He can't see her, and she can't see you. You have to go *now.*"

The Witch's head is bowed, her antlers gouging the earth. Her shoulders shudder, her back curving like a cat's, as her colorless hands come free of the shadows and settle into the sand. She drags herself with curled hands and broken nails, pulling hips and thighs out of the black.

"Long time no see!" the stranger calls, waving at them.

Nova squints, and then he steps back with a soft gasp. "No... Not you... No..." He falls backwards through the fire, and Lucía releases him, snatching a smoldering bit of tinder. She waves it in front of her.

"You can't hurt me in a dream, Lucía. You aren't strong enough."

"I can try."

"You can, but I don't want to hurt *you*...and I will if I have to."

She shakes her head, brandishing her stick. She tries to keep his eyes on her and away from the black figure floating across the sand.

"Nova, wake up. Wake up right now," she hisses. She doesn't dare look away from the stranger. She doesn't know what Nova is doing behind her until she hears the growl, and then he is flying past her—all smoke and ash, fire gleaming in his inky fur, reflecting the stars. She drops her brand and runs after him, but he's so fast, and the Witch is so close...

Nova tackles the stranger, knocking him off his feet, snarling and snapping. Lucía can't see his teeth, only hear their sharp, crocodilian *clack*. The stranger grunts, pushing at his throat and snout, and Nova snaps at him over and over, like an angry rattler. The sand underfoot breaks into rivers of dark red. The cacti blacken and sag, falling in on themselves. Tiny lizards and insects cry out and scramble for the rocks, but the rocks are sinking into the bloody sand. The desert hemorrhages, swells with lava and smoke, and Lucía stumbles, coughing and dancing in place.

"Nova!"

The Witch is almost upon them, and she knows that no matter what, she cannot let the stranger have the Witch, nor the Witch have Nova. She closes her eyes, focusing, and she brings down the stars, catching them in her arms and gathering them against her ribs. She begins to throw them at Nova, flinging them as hard as she can. The stars cut through his swirling form, and he yelps. She continues to pepper him with burning stardust, and the stranger manages to wrestle out from under his murderous cloud.

Lucía dumps the rest of her stars and sprints the last few yards, throwing her arms around Nova's neck. She stares over his shoulder at the Witch, only steps away, reaching towards him with ghoulish hands—

It's too late.

She clutches his cheeks, fingers tugging his fur, and she stares into his strange eyes.

"Wake up, sleepyhead. It's time to get up."

And she is free falling through darkness, the stranger and the Witch and Nova all gone. She gasps, clutching at her throat. Her heart is hammering in her ears. She can't tell if this is the blackness between dreams, or if she has failed, and this is, instead, the blackness of imminent doom.

She screams.

And her eyes pop open—thickly crusted, blinded by the glare of mid-afternoon light. She tries to sit up, but her arms and legs are too weak. Her body feels cold and stiff, unwilling to respond, clotted with atrophy and magic. Her tongue feels fat in her mouth, and her soft plea for help comes out a half-swallowed gurgle. Something rustles in the bushes, black against the sunlight. She peers, trying to make sense of what she's seeing.

The Witch looks almost human in this light—her antlers melting into the scattered pattern of tree limbs overhead.

She cocks her head, and Lucía can see an anemic cheek under her cowl.

"Am I dreaming?"

The Antlers Witch studies her curiously, as though discovering some unexpected strain of mushroom growing on the rocks below.

"I'm awake."

Awake, for the first time in a very long time. She tries again to push herself upright, but her muscles are slack, and the magic is already settling over her once again, heavy and inescapable. She opens her mouth to protest, but the Witch leans over her rock, sprawled on her chest like a mermaid. She opens her pale lips, murmuring something, and her cold fingertips settle on Lucía's brow. She is so very cold. Lucía shivers, fighting the swell of lethargy.

"No, no... Maya..."

Maya, find me...

iv. mason

*(walking through the rain,
i tasted you in my shame,
we're the cocktail that'll mess you up,
a little too much bang for your buck)*

"Fetch, Whale. Go get it."

Whale's right brow lifts, but the terrier remains lying by the front door. He wags his tail just a little for Mason's benefit, but it seems he's done with fetch for the day. Mason wonders if dogs become depressed the way people do. He wonders if Pea misses him as much as Whale misses Nova. Upstairs, Nova is still asleep, still disoriented in the brief moments he's been awake, leaving Mason to wait.

It's weird living at the L. The Libra pack has assured him that it's fine—they have guest rooms for this reason—and they were nice enough to give him the room next to Nova's. They've been nice in a lot of ways: making big breakfasts and dinners, inviting him to play pool and volleyball and go on walks and watch movies, and answering his questions (the ones he can bring himself to ask). They've done this before. But he already knew that from his afternoon chat with Harper about rogue wolves and attacks and choices. This is a shelter for new wolves as much as a recreational space for the pack.

And Mason is a new wolf.

He sighs and goes to collect the rubber ball, peering up at the window of Nova's room. Harper is up there now. Silent, guilty, lost...

And probably still in love with Nova.

Mason snorts, tossing the ball into the air and trying to catch it with his other hand, but he's hopelessly uncoordinated. When they were in high school, Nova picked up juggling for a little while. It'd been way more impressive than Mason could admit at the time, the truth clouded by envy as it often was when Mason was confronted by the sheer ease of Nova's physicality. (There was always envy or longing. Sometimes both.)

He's jealous now, too. Not because Harper is all over Nova when he thinks no one is looking, but because Harper's feelings for Nova seem so simple and earnest. His own are clouded by 20 years of knowing Nova more intimately than anyone else. Mason was there for all his disappointments and his victories, his fears and his quiet joys. He was there when the fault lines formed, and he was there, time and again, to pick Nova up and dust him off when life kicked him down. Twenty years of little envies and secret resentments, unspoken hungers and desperate, sweeping love, and then—at the end of it all—a year and a half of grief and compounded, inexorable abandonment. Nova is his best friend, his first love, his family, and one more person that Mason needed, who dropped him without a fuss.

At least his mom had the decency to do it when he was

six. Nova gave him almost two decades before he let the other shoe drop, and it still hurts. It all hurts.

But Nova is also hundreds of nights of reading under the covers, legs tangled between bags of cookies and sour worms; he is the quiet reminder that for every birthday party Mason's mom couldn't make, someone wanted him in this world with a passion that he himself couldn't always muster; Nova is the whirr of bicycle spokes down sunny sidewalks, declaring that summer has arrived and vanquishing the lingering monotony of the school year; he's the comfort of coming inside on a late November day and smelling cookies baking in the kitchen; he's the rumble of an engine speeding down dark highways with nothing but fuzzy snippets of radio humming in the speakers and the breath fogging the windows...

He still dreams about searching for secret doors behind every gate and hedge in the neighborhood, believing (because Nova believed) that there could be magic in their dull suburban world; he remembers stroking Nova's hair for hours in those moments when Saturno really got to him, whispering stilted encouragements (and—because it was Nova—meaning every clumsy word); he daydreams about the first time they held hands at a restaurant, the way they were too shy to look at each other, sitting side by side and staring at their plates for half an hour, just squeezing each other's fingers back and forth...

Mason was stupid to come here. He's opened the flood-gate. He's allowed himself to want what he wants without restriction, and he *wants* Nova to wake up, to ask him for forgiveness, so that he can say it's all fine, and then he can take Nova home, and they'll start over again and do it right and it'll be the ending they *deserve*. This time, they'll be what the other person needs. This time, they'll try harder to figure out what that need is.

But he's not naive; he already knows it's futile.

Nova loves him, but there is something chasing him—something that Mason has never really understood despite his general expertise in all things Nova. It's something he can't put a name to, can't discern its shape, or hear its voice. And so it's easier to focus on his feelings of abandonment, because he doesn't know what to call the thing that clouds Nova's eyes and drags him deep inside. He is afraid that he's already looked the problem in the eye and failed to recognize it for what it is; he's afraid of the deficits within himself that he hasn't noticed. He doesn't know what kind of monster is hounding Nova, so he doesn't know how to make it go away. Instead, he clings to the idea that Nova is simple: that it was a case of cold feet, a fear of commitment—something disappointing, but pedestrian enough to be safe and understood.

It's easier to blame Nova. Case in point, if it weren't for Nova, he wouldn't be here right now. He wouldn't have been bitten. If he hadn't come here, he wouldn't be contemplating his new life as a freaking *wolf*. This is what he gets for trying to save Nova, who never asked for his help, who got *himself* into this mess, who—

He jumps as the ball comes sailing at his chest, catching it against his breastbone by sheer accident. He looks up, and Manu smiles, pulling his hair under a snapback to keep it out of his eyes.

"Hi. You look scowly."

"H-hi," Mason replies, face going hot. "I'm just...thinking."

"Fair enough," Manu says, offering a lopsided smile. He nods for Mason to follow, heading down the dirt path curving around the outside of the lodge.

"Whale! Whale, come," Mason calls.

Whale does not come, though, and he sighs. At least it seems unlikely the dog will run away. He turns and follows Manu around the house. There's a surprisingly well-built playground in the back, crowned by an elaborate jungle gym at its center. The sun glints off the tops of swings and slides and in the ribs of the monkey bars. It reminds him of preschool, of the day he met Nova...

∘ ∘ ∘

He'd wanted to play on the monkey bars, scuttle up the slide, take a spin on the tire swing, but there were too many kids climbing all over the jungle gym, and they were noisy and unfamiliar, and he was too scared to assume he could play with them and too petrified to ask if it would be okay. So, feeling sorry for himself, he'd crept inside the schoolhouse.

With no one inside, the space felt cavernous and foreboding. His eyes skated rows of tables, folded up nap mats, cubbies stuffed with backpacks and lunch bags, and the big television on its metal stand—everything blue and cold in the darkened room.

He considered playing with blocks under one of the tables until everyone came back in. The other boys had hogged the blocks all morning, and he'd been just as intimidated then, so he hadn't had a chance to pour them onto the floor and sift through the merry blue and red rectangles. But if the teachers caught him, they might yell at him, and they were strangers, too. His mom had told him teachers were nice—that they were only there to take care of him—but he'd seen one of them yell at a group of girls earlier for getting up during sitting down time. She'd sounded like a mountain troll, and he couldn't trust that she wouldn't turn on him if she found him inside when everyone was supposed to be outside.

He retreated to the bathroom to hide until recess was over, except it wasn't empty. An especially runty kid was standing on the toilet seat, leaning against the wall. Mason stopped, surprised—wondering what the boy was up to— and that's when he noticed the marker in his small fist. He let out a loud, scandalized gasp. The boy stilled, and then leaned back, looking over his shoulder with narrowed eyes.

"What do you want?"

Mason flinched, pressing against the door.

"Are you gonna tattle?" the boy asked, hopping from the toilet and stuffing the marker (uncapped) into the waistband of his shorts. "Are you?"

He stomped across the tiles to stand before Mason, looming without looming—managing to be menacing at an inch below Mason's eye level. "Say something, or I'll hit you." He dropped onto his heels, and then he poked Mason in the chest, hard. *"Talk."*

"W–why are you in here?" Mason squeaked.

The boy looked away, turning pink. "Nunnaya beeswax."

"We're supposed to be outside," Mason whispered.

The boy's look hardened, and his throat flexed. "I don't wanna play with them."

That at least made sense. Mason didn't want to be with the other kids either, but he also didn't want to be trapped in the bathroom with this weirdo. He glanced through the crack between door and frame, searching for a place to retreat to—a table, a closet, *anything*—but there was nothing close enough, and he didn't want to turn his back on the kid and end up tackled (or hit).

"Do you have a name?"

Mason shook his head, and his face immediately went bright red—embarrassment running so hot, he could feel sweat prickling on his chest and at the back of his neck.

"That's weird. Why didn't your parents name you?" the boy asked, making a great and agonizing study of his mortified face. Mason willed the boy to look away, to step away, to just leave him alone...

"You're as red as a tomato...or a lobster. Do you wanna be called 'Lobster'?"

"No," he muttered into his collarbones.

"Tell me your name then."

He stared down at their feet. His own shoes were generic white rubber and faux leather, but the angry boy was wearing *purple* shoes with rainbows.

"Those are girls' shoes," he blurted out.

He'd meant to say it to himself, but it was too late.

The kid's eyes were big—doll-like—but right then they were narrowed on Mason dangerously, and he pressed himself flat against the now-shut door. The boy grabbed him, jerked him forward by the collar of his shirt, and Mason swallowed a gasp. Wide-eyed, he looked into the green-bronze eyes of the boy-in-girl's-shoes. They were not friendly.

"You gotta problem, Lobster?"

"Don't call me that."

"My shoes are great. They've got cool colors."

He didn't think he could get any redder, or burn any hotter, but he did, and sure enough, the heat sank into his eyes. He blinked furiously, willing it away. He didn't want to cry in front of some kid in rainbow shoes. He didn't want to cry on his first day of preschool. Dad told him going to school was a step towards being grown up, and grown ups didn't cry. His dad never did, even when he was really sad. (Even when Mom yelled at him.) The boy released him, and he stumbled.

"Nothing to say, huh?"

Mason slumped against the door, a hot swell of tears breaking over his cheeks, and the boy abruptly froze, staring down at him with a confused look, like he didn't understand what he was seeing. Mason curled over his knees, trying to hide in the space behind his thighs.

"You're crying," the kid whispered and dropped to a crouch in front of him, poking his toe. "I'm not really gonna hit you. I swear. Don't cry. Please?"

But now that he'd started, the entire stress of the morning unraveled: he could feel tears dripping onto his shorts; a thick, muddy sound broke from his throat; and his shoulders shuddered with the attempt to repress further emotion.

"I'm sorry. I'm super sorry. I won't call you Lobster anymore. I won't. Please don't cry."

The kid's hands went to his shoulders, pressing down

uncomfortably as he attempted to peek into the hiding space Mason has fashioned for himself.

"Fudgey fudgin'... Hold on."

The pressure relented, and Mason curled deeper, hoping against hope that the kid would just leave him alone, but the boy flopped down in front of him, followed by the clatter of plastic.

"Look, I have markers."

Mason flinched as the cold, wet tip of a marker streaked up his wrist. He looked up, sniffing. "Don't do that."

"What's your favorite thing in the world?"

He stared at the big-eyed kid, rubbing his nose with the back of his wrist and then his face with the inside of his shirt. "Frogs."

The boy drew himself to his knees, rifling through his markers, which weren't even in their box, and pulled out a green one, leaning over Mason's foot. Mason opened his mouth, but swallowed his protest, feeling curious and a little tingly. The kid hunkered over his foot, perfecting an oval before drawing two little circles and lines for feet, and Mason shivered, goosebumps running down his spine in an oddly pleasant way. He rubbed his nose, leaning his chin on his knee, and watched as the kid drew something frog-like on his shoe.

"It doesn't have eyes."

"I'm getting to that."

The boy uncapped the black marker, tongue poking out of the corner of his mouth as he carefully added two dots and a smile. Mason rubbed his forearm, feeling the soft hairs flatten under his fingers and then pop right back up.

"Will you play on the slide with me?" he mumbled.

The boy looked up, tongue retreating into his mouth. Then he smiled. It was so bright, so surprisingly warm, that Mason couldn't quite look him in the face.

"Okay, but tell me your name first."

"Mason."

He looked up, meeting the boy's grin.

"I'm Nova."

o o o

Mason swallows all that residual nostalgia and rubs his eyes. Half-filled hearts pass through his vision. Manu settles onto a swing and kicks, soaring backwards into the air, and Mason shuffles over to a slide that's too narrow for even his shapeless butt. He crams himself in sideways and tries not to look too mournful.

"I didn't have a clue," Manu says, lifting his legs as the swing rocks back and forth, decelerating incrementally. "Not a clue that I had all these wolves around me. I was hanging out in my backyard with my little brother, and this wolf comes out of the woods. My brother managed to get inside, but it got a hold of me, and my aunt came out and shot at it, chased it back into the trees. I went to school, and Oren just looked at me and said, 'Oh.' So we skipped and went walking around the neighborhood. He told me about being a wolf. Then he told his mom about me getting attacked, and the pack went and found the wolf that bit me. I don't know what they did with him. They didn't just do it for me, but they also did, y'know? So who was I to ask?" Manu puts his feet down, stopping the swing, and pulls up his shirt, revealing puckered scars along his ribs. "I was scared, trying to figure out how I was supposed to live my life when once a month I became a wolf who wanted to bite people."

"Did you have to give it up? Your dreams?" Mason asks softly, screwing the toe of his shoe into the dirt.

"I was 16, so I didn't have a whole lot of plans yet. It was all stuff like, *ask Mayhem to the homecoming dance, buy a Porsche, learn to play drums*...and I really only cared about one of those things anyway," he says, smiling down at his knees. "Libra takes care of its own. Besides, we have good relationships with a lot of packs in the Northeast, which means we're taken care of in a lot of spaces. So I went to school, and now I'm studying to be a vet, and I managed to finally ask Mayhem out. The Libra elders made us the youth leaders of the pack, and life is good—maybe even better than it would have been. I don't want to sound cheesy, but if you learn to love lemonade, life can be your favorite drink."

Mason snorts, looking down at his hands. "I write stories for mobile games. It's a small studio, but we won an award last year for a game I helped write, and I was just promoted. I'm supposed to go back home, and now I don't know what will happen. Harper said it's bad to be a lone wolf, but I live in a city. What if I attack people? I have to learn how to do this. I need time, but what if I get fired for taking too much time? I don't know what to do. And I miss my frog."

"Your frog?"

He nods. "His name is Pea. He's with Nova's parents right now. Can a wolf even own a frog? I don't want to eat Pea."

Manu laughs, kicking him lightly on the shin. "Your frog will be fine. *You* will be fine."

"Nova never seemed like he was mad at Maya for biting him. He came here and met Harper, and the three of them were best friends. I thought he was never going to come back. Then one day, he was at my doorstep, and I thought: *He's finally mine.* But I guess Nova has never really been anyone's."

"Well...people *don't* belong to other people," Manu replies. "That's not how it works."

Mason sighs again. "I know, but even so, I felt safe when I thought of myself as *his* person. Then he left, and I just watched him go. I'm mad at him. I'm mad at him for leaving me like that. Maybe if he'd been— Maybe if things were different, I wouldn't have chased him out here. I just... I'm sorry. I'm being shitty. I know I am, but I blame him. It's easy to blame him, because I blame him for so much already. It just doesn't seem fair that things turned out like this. I only wanted to help him."

Manu kicks off, pushing himself into a slow arc. "Do you regret it? Coming here? Trying to help?"

Mason crosses his ankles, trying to find a comfortable spot without lying on the slide. "He's my best friend. How could I? That's why I know I shouldn't blame him, that I'm just using him as an excuse. There's so much I need to say to him, that I want him to say, and...and he's up there, *just—*" He closes his eyes, letting himself collapse against the slide after all. "Is this my fault? Maybe if I had held on tighter, we'd still be together. He wouldn't have been alone, hundreds of miles away, when they came for him. No one would have hurt him. So maybe this *is*... You know?"

"It isn't your fault that bad people exist, or that bad things happen. But how they sculpt you, that's on you. I think you already know you need to stop blaming him. You also need to let go of the idea that it's your fault. I mean, I'm pretty sure Harper has already filled our moping quota. Focus on the good things, like how you came all the way out here and waded into a pack of wolves to try to save your best friend. That means something, you know? It means you're brave— maybe braver than you think. Sometimes when you're brave, you get hurt, but the thing about bravery is that you don't stop because of that. And you know what? It feels good when you know that's who you are, because it means you're strong in the ways that really matter." Manu puts heels into the dirt, climbing out of the swing and stretching. He looks up at the L for a long moment, a private smile flickering in his expression, and then offers Mason a hand.

"That's a good way to put it. Thanks. Really," Mason says, taking Manu's hand and peeling himself from the slide. He follows his gaze to the building, wrestles down a pinch of anxiety (of jealousy) that Harper is up there now, that it may be Harper who's there when Nova wakes. It makes him feel small after Manu's kindness. He stares down at his feet.

"Can I ask you something? Why are you being so nice to me?"

Manu throws an arm around his shoulders and chuckles. "Because I *am* nice. Besides, I've been there—there and back again. Harper might hate Libra, but we take care of each other. We're a family—not always perfect, families never are—but we do our best. Now can I ask you something?"

"Sure. What is it?"

"Do you know why Maddox Hirst kidnapped your friend in the first place?"

Mason turns his eyes to the clouds, squinting against the afternoon light. "No. But I think it has something to do with Maya."

"Maya?" Manu frowns. "What would he want with Maya?"

"I don't know," Mason says, shaking his head. "But maybe when Nova wakes up, we'll have a few more pieces of the puzzle."

∘ ∘ ∘

"Can we stop avoiding each other now?"

Harper jumps, coffee trickling over the rim of his mug.

"Sorry." Mason walks around the bed to sit beside him, trying to push the corgi out of the way.

"You'll never win," Harper mutters into the coffee cup. "Just take what you can get."

Mason manages to shimmy partially onto the bed, the corgie's back paws pressed into his hip. Nova shifts under the covers, but doesn't wake. Whale sleeps beneath his chin, and the border collie has stretched itself along his back. He looks well-guarded at least.

"What are their names again?"

"Abbott is the nice one. Costello is the one trying to push you off the bed."

"Cool. Will you stop pretending I'm not here now?"

Harper lets out a long, overtaxed sigh and tries to stuff

himself into the dark recess of his mug, but the laws of physics remain on Mason's side, and he finally puts his drink down.

"Can we do this outside?" Harper mumbles.

"I don't really know what you think 'this' is going to be, but sure."

They leave the dogs framing Nova, Whale eyeing the others with a brittle, wary expression. Mason wonders if the dogs will be okay—it doesn't seem like Whale wants to share—but Harper seems to know dogs, and he doesn't hesitate, shutting the door softly behind them. He walks out into the parking lot in front of the lodge, getting into his truck.

"You aren't going to abandon me at a bar again, are you?" Mason asks, frowning up through the open window.

"No." Harper stares down at him expectantly, and Mason sighs, climbing into the cab after him. The engine turns over, and a burst of shoegaze grunge sighs from the speakers. Harper turns red, turning the radio off with a very purposeful twist of his fingers. Mason schools his expression, putting on his seatbelt.

They drive away from the lodge, away from town, and into the backroads surrounding the park. It's all greening annuals, black pines, pastures housing dirty little horses, and sagging metal barns.

"This place would be great in the fall. Feels like Halloween in summer."

Harper leans deeper into his seat, his elbow resting on the window ledge. "It's okay, if you like hayrides and corn mazes. There's nowhere to go trick-or-treating, though."

"You've never been?"

"Just at school. We'd get to dress up and trick-or-treat in the afternoon. There was a party in the cafeteria. A band from the high school would come and play really off-tempo versions of all your October favorites."

Mason laughs softly, closing his eyes against the warm air rushing through the window. "We got to dress up at school, too. But movies always make autumn look like this, so there was always this disconnect for me, I guess—like we were getting some off-brand version of Halloween."

"Well, you never know. You might still be here in October," Harper says, eyes on the road.

Mason watches the fields rolling by, bright in that early summer shade of green, broken by stretches of mud and the looming curves of hay bales. There are a couple of kids climbing one to the dismay of a frustrated black lab. Mason watches them in the side mirror until they're gone, smiling to himself.

"I didn't think you'd like it out here in the sticks."

"It's like the start of a fantasy novel, only with less swords and trolls trying to burn Main Street."

"We've got wolves and witches, I guess, but all of them live basically the same as you," Harper says, pulling a pair of white sunglasses from the visor and slipping them on.

"Am I going to be—" Mason stares down at his hands, clamped together, each finger squeezing the blood out of the fingers next to it. "He's the one who bit me, right? The white one—that was *him*?"

"Yeah, that was him."

For a moment, a reckless longing to open the door and

fall out of the truck, to *run* back to the West Coast on his own two legs, surges over him, and he presses his hands between his thighs.

"Am I a beta, too?"

Harper's knuckles clench the steering wheel. His mouth whitens between the press of his lips. "I don't know. I don't know how it works. Obviously I didn't know shit before, so I'm going to just go ahead and learn from that trauma and say I don't know shit now."

"If I am, that makes me... I'll be, um, a threat to Nova."

The truck slows just a little—abruptly enough that his stomach does a minor flip—but Harper quickly compensates, foot smashing down on the accelerator.

"He'll be okay. He has lots of friends," Mason says softly, trying to sound consoling, but this only elicits a deep, unhappy sigh from Harper. "What?"

"He doesn't really."

"You're joking, right? Have you ever looked at his social? There are like a thousand—"

"Not the same thing as a friend. A lot of people like Nova. Not many people are his *friend*," Harper replies, pulling to the side of the road before an old bridge.

"Explain," Mason says, feeling tired—tired of worrying which one of them is the problem, tired of worrying about Nova, and tired of navigating Harper's defenses.

Harper takes his keys from the ignition, drapes them over his thigh, and leans back. Behind the sunglasses, his eyes look nearly black.

"Someone might like you, but that doesn't mean they're going to be there for you. They can love hanging out with you at happy hour, but that doesn't mean they're going to understand if you call them at two in the morning. In fact, the more people *like* you, the more likely they are to want you to be nothing *except* the things they like about you. But most people like being liked, so when they feel someone wants them around—and people *will* want you around if you're giving them something—they try to please that person. They bend over backwards. You end up used, and used is not loved. Do you get that? *Nobody* has a lot of friends."

They sit in the silent truck, watching the river rushing under the blackened skeleton of the old bridge, and Mason tries to make sense of Harper's perspective. He tries to imagine how being well-liked could be bad.

At his silence, Harper continues, softer now: "'Friend' is another word for 'family.' Friends are the people who are more worried about *how* you are and *why* you're calling them at whatever hour than annoyed. Friends are the people who really see you, who care about you enough to realize you're fucked up enough that you need to call in the first place, and who love you through that."

It feels like a many-legged something is circling his guts. Mason swallows thickly, his face burning. "Do you think— Am I Nova's friend? By those standards?"

"Well, you're here, so probably," Harper replies, staring at him like he's suggested the sky is purple. "But I guess only you would know how deep that goes."

He searches for something to stare at besides his hands, his lap, the bridge, or Harper. Squeezing his eyes shut, he manages to whisper, "It would be good if Nova had more friends like that—like you."

"You're the one who jumped into a pit of fighting wolves to save him."

"It's what he would do."

"I know." Harper almost smiles, flicking his glasses up his brow and pinning his gaze on Mason. His eyes, like Nova's, seem almost too large for his face, an indigo kind of blue, darkly hooded, and cold. It's like looking into deep water, he thinks to himself, trying, but failing, to escape Harper's pointed stare.

"I guess if you have shit you don't feel good about, now's as good a time as any to figure that out and do what you can about it."

He glances up at Harper, nodding once.

"I don't want to give you love advice, though. It's contrary to my interests."

"You *do* love him, then?" Mason asks, and Harper looks away, blowing hair from his face.

"Who knows?"

"I think you know. It just depends on how much you're willing to be honest with yourself." He looks down at his hands. "But I'd rather not give you love advice either."

Harper snorts, pushing the glasses back down over his eyes.

They stay, watching the river for a few more minutes. Mason tries to imagine it taking away all his insecurities—his doubt and his guilt and his fear. He turns them into rocks, lets them drop deep into the brown water—buffeted by the current, by rushing walls of silt and debris, until they're worn down by the river's pressure and gone.

Gone,

gone,

g o n e.

It doesn't really work, but he doesn't feel as jittery when Harper restarts the truck and drives them to the Wawa for coffee and hoagies. Mason buys a box of cheese crackers for the dogs, and they eat half of them before they get back to the L.

"If we *are* both his betas, who's going to look after Nova?" Mason asks as they turn onto the narrow, bumpy road that leads to the lodge.

"Dunno."

"So, what then?" he asks, looking up at the dark pine walls.

"What else? We figure out how to get away from that fuckjack."

Mason opens his mouth, feeling his heart start with something he'd almost lost in the last few days, but then the screen door swings open, and Lupe comes out, waving at them excitedly.

"What is it?" Harper asks, jumping out of the truck, the door slamming behind him.

Mason hurries after him, trying to compress the barrage of feelings battering him from all sides.

Lupe, pink-faced and breathless, crows, "He's awake!"

v. nova

(bury me in the sand,
let me become a planet for hermit crabs;
don't wait for me)

Whale whines, hovering above his face, licking eyes and
cheeks until he thinks he's drowning. He groans, a long,
blurry sound that precipitates the shift from side to belly.
He buries his face in the mattress, but the dog is not
deterred. Rather, he's joined by a heavier dog who waddles
up to Nova, sniffing his ears—belligerently oblivious to the
snap of tension in Whale's spine. Nova tries to roll away
from the barrage of dog breath, but there's another one
tucked against him on the other side—black and fluffy and
doleful. He sits up.

"Where the fuck...?"

Maybe it's the sleep in his eyes. He tries to blink it
away, but he still isn't sure where he is. It's a cabin, but not
desolate or rundown like the camp Fido imprisoned him
in. Here he's surrounded by rich log walls, framed crayon
drawings, and fresh linen curtains blowing over a cracked
window. This place is not abandoned; this is someone's

home. He wriggles out from a mountain of quilts and throws. The border collie gets up and gives itself a shake before hopping off the bed. It's a pretty smart dog. It opens the door on its own and trots outside. Back on the bed, Whale runs in unhappy circles around his feet, trying to keep the corgi from sniffing his butt. But that, Nova decides, is a Whale problem.

The pains in his body are kaleidoscopic. Every movement reveals a new shape and hue, so he gingerly scoots to the side of the bed, finding a cup of water and pitcher placed on a tray there. He drinks the water, refills it, drinks it again, and then picks up the pitcher, drinking directly. Too busy guzzling water, he misses the knock and nearly douses himself when he notices the woman lingering in the doorway: short and compact with a dagger-like haircut falling over her left eye. He lowers the pitcher and rubs his chin, finding rough patches of hair sprouting along his jawline. He wonders how long he's been out.

"Hi," she says, waving shyly. "Abbott came to get me, so I— Well, I'm here." She moves to the foot of the bed, looking like she doesn't know how to arrange herself.

He blinks rapidly, feeling grit clinging to his edges, and begins to dig at his tear ducts. "Who are you?"

Whale escapes the corgi, fussing at his side until Nova lifts his elbow and lets him slip underneath. The corgi pads over to the girl, stubby tail wagging hopefully. She puts a hand on its brow and offers a scratch, but this seems to be the wrong answer, because it huffs and hops down to sniff her ankles without much enthusiasm.

"Guadalupe...or just Lupe. You're in Blackpines, New

Jersey, in the Libra pack's lodge. We call it the 'L.'"

"Oh. Am I a prisoner?"

She stares at him and then laughs tentatively. "No? You're free to leave anytime."

He nods, finally extracting the grime from his eyes, and returns his attention to her. She has a cute face—a button nose and small lips, dramatic eyebrows, and darkly rimmed, ochre eyes. She looks like an adult, but she holds herself like a teenager who's afraid the teacher is about to call on her. She doesn't look like she wants to hit him, however, and that's the most important thing.

"Is Harper here? Wait, is Mason here? Is he—" He tries to stand, but his blood has not acclimated to such altitude, and he sways, collapsing back on the bed.

"You okay?"

Again, he nods, rubbing his face until the dots go away.

"They went on an errand an hour or so ago," she says. "They're fine. Well, I mean, mostly fine—"

"What?" he asks, trying to keep the edge out of his voice, dragged down by the weight of fear in his stomach.

"Your friend was bitten. He's recovering, but... Well, you know what comes next."

The curtains rise and fall, mottled by the shadows of leaves. He can see clouds slipping overhead in the thin break above the fabric. He swallows thickly. His throat doesn't loosen. Lupe sits down beside him, putting a hand on his knee, but not saying anything. He nods.

"I fuck everything up," he says at last, trying to keep his voice from shaking. "Yeah. That about sums it up."

"You didn't bite him."

"Sorry, I just..." He stands, wobbly, but not dizzy this time. He goes to the window, pulling back the curtain. "Nevermind, nevermind. It's nothing."

She remains silent, watching his back, and he opens the window a little further.

"Ugh, sorry. I'm making you uncomfortable, and we just met. Normally, people find me way less...this. You are part of the rare Bad First Impression Club. Is Maya here?"

"No, she ran off after we chased that other pack away. You know Maya?"

"Yeah, of course. How do you know her?"

"We went to school together, before she moved to California. We weren't really friends. She didn't know me as Lupe."

"Who did she know you as?"

Lupe shrugs. "A different name. A dead name."

He glances at her again and then nods. "Gotcha."

"How do *you* know her?" she asks.

Nova puts his hands on his back, gives his hips a pop. "I saw a wolf fall into the river. I went in after it, and when I pulled it out, it panicked and bit me. Then it—she— kidnapped me. It was a way better kidnapping experience than this last one. I can't wait to write *that* review. I've got a lot to say about Fido's hospitality."

"Fido?"

"Uh, nothing. Nevermind. So you knew Maya when she was a fetus? Also, do you have food? I need food."

Lupe laughs incredulously, getting to her feet. "We have food. No cotton candy, but other stuff."

"Cotton candy?"

"Harper said you'd want some, but I couldn't find any at the supermarket."

Fragments of green, sparks of bronze, stare back at him from the glass. His mind swells with night-blue walls and the flatness of a mattress on a wooden floor, the smell of plain soap and black coffee, rare smiles hidden behind curling locks of brown hair, and the steady pulse of a heart-beat beating strong against his temple.

I missed you.

> *I fucked you over.*

He sighs. "Of course. Of course, he would."

He tries not to think about how nice it would be to fall into Harper's arms and hide from the Big Bad Wolf *and* the Evil Witch. Harper, skinny as a pole, and yet so solid, so constant...

"I'm a vegetarian," he says, changing the subject. He lifts Whale from the bed and cradles the dog to his chest.

"You're in luck. I'm a grilled cheese artist," she replies, pausing in the doorway. "I'm also good at pancakes. You did just wake up."

He shakes his head. "Grilled cheese is just dandy. Tell me more about baby Maya and Harper."

∘ ∘ ∘

"Harper and Maya were really insular. I don't mean it in a bad way. They weren't mean. Just that they were attached at the hip, and they didn't hang out with anyone else if they could help it. Maya was super shy, and Harper was really serious and kind of volatile, even back then. It was like talking to an adult, you know? You always felt like you were going to get in trouble. Maya hid behind him a lot—or that's what I used to think. But when she left, I think we realized it'd been the other way around all along.

"But Maya was really shy. She never spoke above a whisper, and she hated talking in front of other people. One time, when we were reading in class, the teacher called on her, and she got in trouble for whispering. She started crying, and Harper got up and yelled at Mrs. Matthews. He wound up with in-school suspension for three days. Maya hid in the library until he was back. She was the prettiest girl in class. I admired her a lot. Like, at first I thought I had a crush on her, but I realized later I just wanted to be her—to look like her, to know what it feels like to be someone who looks like that. She had this unbelievable curly hair, and her mom would put it in these perfect little braids. She looked like a princess. And she was so tall and thin and just, you know, pretty. When I first came out, I tried to dress like her. You know, combat boots and tunic dresses and those cute jean jackets with pins and patches all over them... But it didn't look the same on me, and I got over trying to be someone I'm not."

She frees a salt and vinegar chip, popping it into her mouth, and smiles toward the past. Nova looks down at the strings of cheese cascading from his sandwich. She's put apples and chipotle mustard on it. He isn't sure of the cheese, but something fancier than cheddar. She truly is a grilled cheese artist.

He swallows. "You are pretty, though. You don't have to be tall and thin to be pretty."

"Yeah, I know that now. Sometimes the logic doesn't connect with the emotion, but I keep reminding myself anyway. Back then, I couldn't do that. The idea that me looking like me could be okay... I had to go through a lot to realize I'm fine like this."

He nods. Afternoon light moves through the cow print curtains, cuts an orange slice across the counter and her cheek. It catches in her lashes, glimmers in her hair. She looks like the kind of person it would be easy to find *home* with. Someone beautiful and rare. Someone very different from himself. He pushes the thought aside, biting deep into the sandwich.

"Another time, Maya tripped during the school fitness test and hurt her knees, so Harper carried her piggyback to the finish line. I guess she kind of liked being carried around, because she made him keep doing it until the teachers said it wasn't appropriate for girls and boys to touch like that."

Nova snorts, picking the crust off the second triangle. "I wouldn't think it'd be a problem with them."

Lupe reddens. "Well, not for Maya, no. But I think Harper did have a crush on her. I always thought that he likes girls...a little?" It comes out as a squeak, and her face goes maroon. Nova looks away, letting her collect herself.

Huh.

"Um, anyway." She clears her throat and picks at the dark lock falling over her eye before continuing: "They were sent to the principal, and I heard that she straight up said that she didn't like boys. She said the idea of Harper being her boyfriend was gross. She wound up in detention, and Harper wouldn't talk to her for a week. He still ate lunch with her every day, but she'd clearly hurt his feelings. She never said anything like that in front of him again as far as I know, though there was one time when she asked Miranda out... She told Miranda that she'd never been into boys, which I guess was what Miranda wanted to hear—just not in the way Maya was expecting, because then Miranda asked Harper out, and he was... I mean, I think we all knew he liked Maya back then, so he turned her down, so she went around saying he was gay until Maya punched her in the boob. They basically hated each other after that. It became a serious feud. Like, it lasted until she moved to California."

Nova slips his fingers inside the chip bag, feeling around for something better than crumbs, but someone else has plundered this bag well before it was set before him. He sighs, retracting his arm and licking crumbs off the tips of his fingers. "Are you still into Harper?" he asks, glancing at her.

She goes red again. "He's cute, and he's tall. When he smiles, he is really, you know, good looking. I don't know him, though. I don't think many people do. Well, maybe you do."

"Mm," he replies in his best noncommittal hum, and then: "No one ever expects *Maya*. She's like a suckerpunch personified. If you fool yourself into thinking she isn't paying attention, or that she's too shy or introverted to disagree with you, she will put you in your place. I like that about her, though. She's not a mean or a hard person, but she maintains her boundaries. I've never been good about that. My boundaries get trampled, and I become ugly and stupid. I act like someone else entirely, and I— Well, anyway, she's everything you see *and* everything you don't."

"Most people are," Lupe laughs.

He grins, ducking his head. "You know what I mean. When we first met, she didn't know what to do with me. She bit me, and then she ran away. And then the next thing I know, some girl is standing outside my apartment, and she tells me to get in her car—that it's an emergency—and I wind up in Jersey."

"Why would you get in a car with a stranger who just randomly appears outside your house?" Lupe asks.

"I thought she needed help?"

Lupe shakes her head in disbelief. "Go on."

"We used to go to a diner outside town on Sunday nights. We'd eat fries and chocolate shakes. She would dip her fries into the shake and talk about, well, everything. She talked about growing up here with Harper, about how mad she was when her mom made her move, how she didn't like any of her stepsiblings, and how she was worried, because her girlfriend had dropped out of school to start a band—not because she didn't think the band wouldn't make it, but because she was scared her girlfriend would fall in love with the drummer. She was afraid because her girlfriend had this really intense drive. She had a dream she'd been chasing for years, and Maya was trying to make sense of a Spanish language degree. She'd only picked it up because she wanted to write the girlfriend love poems, but she wasn't very good at poetry."

"What was she good at?"

He hums and rolls his weight onto his forearms, eyes cast skyward. "Decorating, or like, not decorating, but making things to decorate with? When I moved in with her and Harper, I thought they must have a lot of money or something, because the apartment was really nice. There were all these garlands and beautiful frames covered in seashells—" He pauses, squinting. "Never anything *in* the frames, but lots of frames. She would fix up furniture, paint it, and make it really nice. She always had a project going on."

It had been immediately obvious: the apartment was *Maya's* domain. Harper had put up some curtains in his room, but he never even bought a frame for his bed, and his furniture was the featureless plastic stuff that every high-end container store promised college students would love, if not desperately need. Maya was the one who'd rooted around secondhand shops to find the perfect three-legged almost-antique coffee table, she was the one who'd painted the ends of the curtains gold, and she was the one who'd covered the refrigerator with magnetic poetry and crude rest stop magnets.

She filled the kitchen with not just tupperware, but tupperware in *color*; she scoured the post-summer sales to secure the most economical and brightest pieces for the kitchen. She made garlands to hang from every corner and framed their mismatched collegiate art collections in homemade frames. She repainted a dining room table, a bed frame, cabinets, until everything was dreamlike and colorful and comfortable—like something from a children's book.

And she'd left it all behind without a second glance.

He wipes a trail of crumbs and grease from his cheek. "She'd hang out in the living room, watching movies about girls robbing banks and stuff like that, working and working

THE LIGHT IN HER DREAMS

and working, and when she was done... I mean, Harper and I really benefited from her skills. That place was a lot nicer than it would've been if it was just been the two of us. But she didn't think she'd find sustainable work doing that, especially not if her girlfriend ever had to lean on her. I don't know. The things she made looked like they came from one of those fancy boutique stores. I think Harper kept most of it. I only took a couple of things."

There had been a garland made of gauzy tissue petals. She'd done the lettering herself: *He loves you, he loves you not...* (Neither he nor Harper had ever been brave enough to count the flowers, to see what she had landed on.) A cross-stitch Christmas ornament with three little wolves, which had hung on the fridge, looped around the freezer door. He'd grabbed it almost by accident when he left—*almost*—because it had always been his favorite. It had probably been Harper's favorite, too. That moment in time was bright and peaceful. Happy for them both. But he supposes light comes and goes, and bright moments end, too.

Up and down, up and down. That's life.

He scratches his chin and returns to the story. "She made her own clothes. She'd been doing it since high school. She showed me pictures from a scrapbook she'd made. She was beyond stylish. I mean, if she didn't want to craft, I feel like she could easily have gotten into fashion. Plus, she was a thrift store master. She found a couple of shirts for me— old-school, vintage band shirts. I still have them in my— Fuck."

"What is it?"

"You didn't happen to find a car just sitting around

anywhere, did you? Those fuckers stole my car. I don't know where they stashed it. They better not be driving it around."

"No, sorry. If they hid it in the forest, Harper is your best bet. He knows all the little roads around the park. I'm sure he'd be happy to help you look. Do you want any more of these?"

He shakes his head, and she crumples the broken remnants of the chips, turning to throw them in the bin. Still turned, she asks, "What *is* your relationship? With Harper, I mean. Someone was saying that you two were a thing, and he spent a lot of time watching over you while you were sleeping. I even saw him picking the tangles out of your hair..."

He reaches up, running his fingers through his hair. It's true: it only feels a little knotted.

"*Harper* did that?"

She nods, still not looking at him.

"I would have thought it was Mason. He's always super anal about stuff like that. I guess Mason is angrier than Harper."

"Harper is a pretty sensitive person."

"I know."

"And he has a lot on his plate right now."

Nova runs his hands over his face.

Don't we all?

"I'm sorry," she says. "You didn't ask to be here, but now you are, and so is he..."

He presses the heels of his palms into his eyes, feeling his chest hardening, anxiety creeping in through the gaps in his ribs.

"Yes. We are here. Yes, *indeed*, Mason is here and Harper is here and I am here, and that is not something I would have predicted, and it is certainly not something I'm looking forward to, especially if Mason is actively pissed off at me. Honestly, if my car was here, I'd leave before they get back."

"What?"

He drops his hands, laughing weakly.

She frowns and crosses her arms. "I think you owe them more than that. They took care of you—both of them. You can't just... You're joking, right?"

He looks away, lets the bitter laughter die. "Sure. Anyway, I'm not thinking I want to rekindle anything, or lead anyone on. I'm more worried about..."

But he falters, eyes narrowing on a speck of jam dried to the counter. Five minutes ago, he would have told her the sneaking suspicion he has about Lucía's witch, but it doesn't feel safe now. Fear prickles down his sternum, settling heavily in his stomach. He swallows. He needs to get out of here, for his own sake. The idea feels foreign, but the panic knotting up his chest and guts feels very real and urgent. This isn't bullies in the school parking lot, and it isn't Saturno sneering at him from across the dinner table. There's something deep and vast spreading around him, and if he makes one wrong move...

Existential horror. It's existential horror.

"Have you ever been terrified on an existential level?" he blurts out, still staring at the scab of jam, itching to pick at it, already feeling the sticky grain beneath his nails. He lifts his hands, examining them. There probably isn't space for jam with all the dirt in there.

"Are you okay?"

"Not really. I need a shower," he says, sliding off the stool. "I can wash the plate. Is it okay if I just leave it here for now? Where's the shower?"

He realizes he's talking in circles; he's left her spinning in his verbal dust, unsure of which question to answer or where to start. He waits for her to catch up, tuning out the steady acceleration of his heart.

Slow down. Be slow.

Whale whines, wagging his tail in a low, anxious arc, and Nova tries not to be mad at himself for making Whale worried. He scrubs his face again.

"I just need a shower. Is that okay?"

"Yeah. Yeah, of course. It's down the hall."

"Okay, thanks." He turns, following the trajectory of her finger. He can feel himself doing an agitated half-hop thing with his left leg, but the idea of being alone is too immediately appealing to allow for self-consciousness. He stops short of sprinting for the showers, turning the corner just as the sound of tires on gravel comes murmuring through the windows. He stumbles over his own feet, half-frozen.

Behind him, he hears Lupe hurrying to the front door. Her voice is bright and urgent when she calls out, and he gives up any hope of escaping to the showers. He turns, a man facing his sentence—unhappy, but submissive—and creeps back into the kitchen to watch as Harper's dark head bobs up the steps. He has just enough time to reach down and scoop Whale into his arms before Harper squeezes past Lupe, Mason hot on his heels. He abruptly stops, and Mason bumps into him, and with the two spare dogs jumping around, and Lupe trying to get out of the way, it becomes a massive pile-up.

From the tangle of people and dogs, Harper and Mason stare at him like he's the prettiest rainbow unicorn they've never seen. He almost laughs, because their expressions are so similar, and the whole smash of people and dogs in the doorframe feels absurdly slapstick, but he just stands there, hugging Whale and watching apprehensively.

No one else says anything.

That's always been his job.

He clears his throat and half-smiles. "Hi."

vi. maya

(if you connect the lines between the stars,
they become a web;
but you know: where there's a web, there's a spider)

"Were you digging holes again?"

"What do you mean?"

"You *know* what I mean, Maya."

When she was a kid, Dogeared was her favorite place in the world—the mismatched green and yellow furniture, the walls of books stacked floor to ceiling and often double-rowed (she always felt bad for the books in the back, always wondered if anyone else ever pulled the front row aside to see them), the dog paintings and accessories, and, of course, the living, breathing wagging pups. Her dad was allergic, so they never had a family pet, but on Saturday mornings, her mom would bring her into town and leave her at Dogeared while she went to the salon or to buy groceries, and Maya would sit in the window seat upon a throne of cushions with the owner's beagles gathered around her like dolls, and she would read aloud to them about bigger, braver dogs.

All those beagles are gone now. In their place there's a

scruffy jack russell sitting in a canary armchair, chewing a thickly knotted rope. She taps on the window, but it doesn't look up.

"I needed money," she replies, and Bruno sighs into the mouthpiece, blistering her eardrums. She frowns at her reflection, scratching a bit of mud from the edge of her jaw. "Do you have to do that?"

"You could try a bank."

"I don't have an address."

She moves on to picking at the garden soil under her nails. They spent the night digging in her dad's backyard, unearthing the babysitting-ice-cream-scooping-lawn-mowing funds she'd squirreled away in the summers of her adolescence—money she'd saved in case she and Lucía ever had to run away to Canada.

Her dad doesn't live in Blackpines anymore. He fled north when they moved to San Francisco—a two hour drive, which would have been a pain in the ass if they'd had to hitchhike again, but Jude unearthed Nova's car sometime around three in the afternoon, so they'd gone joyriding for a few hours (windows down, music blaring) before letting his wallet take them out for burgers (she figured saving his life was worth a thank-you burger or two), and then they'd set out for her dad's house.

"Your ma called mine."

"Mmmmmm," she replies, squinting and bringing her nails closer.

Nova's homescreen didn't have a lock on it, just an overflowing log of texts and phone calls. She'd scrolled through them briefly, but most of it was his boys and his moms worrying over him.

She'd taken pity on the moms and sent them a quick, [call you soon]

If it were anyone else, she might worry about lying, but back at uni, Nova had called his house at least once a week, so by her reckoning, he's probably already talked to them. No harm, no foul.

"I don't really care," she continues, gnawing at her nail, but it only pushes the grit deeper.

"Maya, it's been three years. I know they handled things badly, but they didn't mean it like *that*."

She spits, cringing at the mineral sharpness between her teeth. "I'm close—closer than ever. I know I'll find her soon."

"Maya, maybe it's time to—"

"Don't say it. Do not say it. You're the only one who's ever believed in us. You're the only one who hasn't given up. So don't give up on her, Bruno. *Don't*."

His sigh is softer this time, directed away from the receiver. "Lo siento, Maya."

They remain quiet for a long moment, listening to the other breathing. Bruno is probably sitting in his car in front of the office, the big tooth over the door casting a shadow across his hood. He's probably looking into the rearview mirror, staring into his own worried eyes, his straight nose and firm mouth cast in elegant relief.

Bruno Mendoza: too awkward to be a heartthrob, too handsome to be a dork. Lucía's little brother by blood, Maya's through time.

But it's always been easy for her to think of the Mendozas as family. Her heart is ambivalent with her stepsiblings and resentful towards her stepparents, but when she thinks about Bruno and Jimena, she feels a quiet, tender pining. She has loved them and envied them, fought with them and learned with them. *They* are what she misses about San Francisco now—the family she wishes she'd had.

Her mom remarried and filled her life with Starlings: three bratty stepsiblings and a know-it-all stepdad who never approved of anything she did, from the Bs and Cs on her report cards to the dresses she wore to Lucía's house. She was the only Douglas in those walls, and she felt it. Her singularity was palpable, and every day, she contended with it: how they outnumbered her, how she wasn't really one of them...

And things weren't any better with her dad. She was forced to visit Jersey every summer, but they never let her go to Blackpines or see Harper. She'd fly out in July, and her dad would make her watch Javier and Jaime practically the whole time—keeping her estranged from both Lucía *and* Harper. Sure, he was glad to see her. Why wouldn't he be? Her arrival meant a month of free babysitting while he and Marta went out and did whatever old people do for fun. She imagines it was something to do with stamp collecting. She refuses to consider that it might have been sex.

But when she was at the Mendozas, she was home. The Mendozas made time for each other, they rolled with the punches, and they took their lumps together. They accepted her—even the bad parts.

She'd called Trella 'Abuelita' alongside the rest of the grandkids, knew Lucía's mom as 'Mama Linda' and her dad as 'Papa Bonbon,' had always thought of Jimena as 'hermanita,'

and she'd never struggled to see Bruno as a best friend and
brother. He was the first person they came out to. He kept
their secret and stood beside them when Lucía decided to
put it to the rest of the family. He paved the way for them—
ensured that Maya was loved not just as an extra daughter,
but as Lucía's person.

If Maya's mom had been less focused on the little kids, on
her husband, on her picture books; if her dad had let her be
a kid instead of rebranding her as an adult the moment it
was convenient for *him*... Maybe then she would have come
out before Lucía was taken. Maybe it would be easier to
believe Bruno when he says, "They worry about you. They
love you. Maya, they *want* to help you, to make it up to you.
If you just called them—"

"I don't have a phone."

"But you called me."

"Because I love you."

He's quiet for a moment, trying not to judge, but the
disapproval is thick in the silence, and she sighs.

"I love them, too. I do. But they don't support me. They
can't support me, because they don't understand me."

"And you gave them a ton of chances to fix that, right?"

Her teeth snap together, closing on the tip of her tongue,
and she flinches. "You're being an asshole."

"I'm being honest."

She runs the tip of her tongue along the inside of her
teeth, wincing at the sting, and turns from the bookstore,
wandering across Main Street to the bakery on the other
side. There used to be a sign with cupcakes on it—*Perfection
in Confection*. It looks like they've redone the roof and done

away with the sign, replacing it with a chic blackboard by the door. She kicks it lightly.

"Bruno, I *cannot* deal with them right now. I can't hold their hands while they come to terms with everything. Why am I the one you're calling unfair?"

"They weren't upset because you are gay, Maya. They were upset because you hid it for so long."

"I only have time for Lucía." She turns away as a couple comes through the door, listening to their retreating footsteps before speaking again. Her voice is low and raw when she says, "The only thing I can do right now is look for her. If they really want to help me, if they really care about me, they'll respect that. They'll wait until I come to them."

Bruno is silent, but she thinks this time it's not because he thinks she's a jerk. She smiles to herself, though it doesn't feel like much of a victory.

"At least let them know you're okay? With your own voice? Please, Maya?"

She sucks down a sigh, closing her eyes.

"Imagine how much better it will be when you find her— both of our families finally celebrating together."

"That's not fair."

But even so, the image is already in her head: a backyard full of Christmas lights and streamers, Lucía and Esteban strumming their guitars side-by-side, her stepdad tossing burgers, Jimena and Calla chatting about the boys they met at university, and her mom, smiling at her smiling at Lucía. Maybe she'll lean over and tell Mama Linda that they look beautiful together. Maybe she'll put them in one of her stories.

Lucía's disappearance released an avalanche that rolled over all their lives. It was revelatory and brutal, and it tore away every hiding place and barrier, leaving them in the blinding morning light, half-drowned in confusion and grief.

She clearly remembers the moment her mom finally put the pieces together. She'd stared at Maya as though they'd never met before, and everything that had come out of her mouth had been uncurated and sharp. She'd made everything about her, but it *wasn't* about her. It was about Maya and it was about Lucía and her mom's reaction wasn't right. A mother shouldn't be so selfish, not when her child is the one in traction. There is no part of Maya that does not believe this.

But it *would* be nice...to be with her mom, in the center of that happy family—everyone finally together. If she could look at Maya and know her and love her for what she is (and what she isn't)...

She sighs, making it sound three times as exasperated as she feels, just so he knows it's a *capital* F favor.

"I'll try," she says, putting her back to the door and pushing inside. "But I have to go. Tell them not to worry about holes. I'll find her soon, and we'll come home. No more need for holes."

He's nodding. His scruff scratches the receiver, and she wishes—deeply, bitterly—that she could put her arms around his neck and hold him. She closes her eyes and imagines the minty, crisp note of his aftershave. It would be so nice to just hug him, to feel safe and stable and wanted...

"Okay," he says. "Okay, Maya. Okay. Te quiero."

"Te quiero, Bruno," she repeats softly.

They breathe, and then she hangs up.

She buys two chocolate croissants and two lattes, and then heads back outside to find Jude rooting around in the trunk. The rear of the hatchback juts skywards, curiously obscene. She meanders across the street, placing a paper cup on the bumper and slipping a croissant into Jude's mouth. Jude starts, making a soft *mfph* around the pastry, and looks up. She doesn't seem guilty about going through Nova's earthly belongings with abandon.

Maya looks down at the mess, feeling similarly unbothered. She should care, she thinks. This stuff belongs to Nova, and she cares about Nova—enough to do really stupid things to protect him, as it turns out—but there's a disconnect somewhere, and *that* unsettles her more than the pillaging.

"Anything good?" she asks, reaching for a pair of hot pink sunglasses only to find one of the nose pads gone. She slips them on anyway, tilting them into place.

Jude holds up a shirt that looks about a hundred-thousand washes too old, holes peppering the threadbare cotton with a hand-drawn skull scrawled beneath some obscure band name. It's hard to read (*Something-Eye?*), but she remembers this one: a Christmas present from back then. That's Nova's, she thinks. That's one she wants him to keep. She puts it back, reaching into the camo duffel to unearth a Black Flag tee. Lucía would like it, she thinks, and Lucía will need clothes when they find her, so she takes it, throwing it over her shoulder.

She stuffs the remaining croissant into her mouth, tossing the waxy bag into the mess, and joins Jude in rooting through his things. It's both more and less than she would expect. It looks like he was either in the middle of traveling, or maybe living out of his car, when the Anathema caught him. She hopes it was the former.

They find a bright red toothbrush with a kid's movie hero on the handle, some kind of organic deodorant that smells oddly herbal (*he didn't used to smell like that*), a camping stove, an assortment of dollar store chargers, a sleeping bag that reeks a little too much of what Nova smells like under that eco deodorant, cans of dog food and vegetable soup (and Fruity Pebbles, *of course*), an old plastic lunch box full of makeup, and a cardboard box that feels less utilitarian and more like the stuff of home: there's a child's rosary; post-cards from grandparents in Phoenix; rusting license plates from Oregon and Nevada and, unexpectedly, New Jersey; a white coffee mug with *Mason* scrawled in fancy letters; and an envelope full of photos: one of the her and Harper sitting in the kitchen (her in a camisole and running shorts; Harper in just his boxers) looking fashionably unassuming, several featuring his moms and a boy with reddish-brown hair rolling his eyes at the camera, and one of Harper just looking out the apartment window against the sunset—sleepy in orange light and navy shadow.

She also unearths a collection of secondhand paperbacks promising stories about summer love (newer, because it's boys and boys and girls and girls on the covers, and she stuffs one of these into the waistband of her shorts) and some odds and ends that she can't easily place: sea glass and dried dandelion; an empty bottle of cologne and a lip balm; odd sketches on lined paper and a couple of movie stubs; and a cache of debris that seem like junk, but must be memories...

She straightens, finishing the croissant, and hums to herself. Not much they can use. Jude sighs, stepping back and stretching her arms behind her. Maya leans over to brush crumbs from the corners of her mouth, and she smiles almost sweetly, lowering her eyes. Sometimes, when she's not being an extraterrestrial, Jude is like this. Maya is never sure what to make of it: is it something she's learned, or does she like Maya? A tool, or the truth? Jude turns to her and repays the favor, and a trill echoes in her belly.

They take their coffees, close the hatch, and go to sit on the blistering hood. Maya wishes she'd gotten them iced lattes instead, but Jude doesn't complain, sitting uncomfortably close in the afternoon heat.

"We should get our hair done while we're here," Maya says, blowing steam from her cup.

Jude stares at her, running her fingers through her hair. It's reached the point of unwashed that almost looks clean, except that it sits so flat on her head it makes her look like a dead thing.

"Well, I might. It needs some love. Do you want to wait at the bookstore?"

"No," Jude says. A black bird comes beating down, settling in a nearby tree and sending a couple of pigeons frantically flapping away. Jude turns to it, smiling. "Where did you get them?" she asks, holding up her cup, and Maya nods towards the bakery across the street. "Oh. He wants bread, I think." She swallows the rest of her latte, and Maya takes the cup, stacking it below her own.

"Just don't wait in the car," Maya says, shaking her head and sliding off the hood with a squeak. The back of her thighs sting, and she rubs them, trying to diffuse the heat to no avail.

Someone whistles, and she turns, smelling wolf.

"You," they say at the same time, and Maya goes a wary kind of silent.

Caleb Greer and Angus Walsh saunter towards her, trailed by a couple of faces she barely remembers: Haiden Beaux-(Something frail and French) and Carmen Ro-(Something that sounds red, but means something else entirely). Haiden has shaved the sides of her head, her sun-streaked hair wild and falling over her shoulder in dun-brown waves, her angular face sparkling with studs and stones. Carmen looks like she's taken a page out of the same style book, except her thick black hair is slicked into a ponytail, and her face is clear of metal, decorated only with Corvette red lipstick. Maya's toes flex in her boots.

Caleb and Angus look like the same breed of local bar, local brew knuckle-draggers she remembers, and she wonders what Carmen and Haiden are doing with Greer and Walsh, except they all smell of wolf. She wrinkles her nose and wonders how they can stand to be in the same pack as the fucktwins. People have always had funny tastes in Black-pines.

Carmen's cheeks color, and she looks away. Haiden frowns, slipping her fingers between Carmen's (at least they aren't *with* Greer and Walsh—at least there's that), and Maya realizes she's been staring at Carmen's mouth a little too long and turns to watch Jude slide from the hood of the car, standing beside her and looking between the four wolves with only enough interest as to determine whether they are a threat or not. Maya tries to elbow her, but Jude seems to be in that implacable place where she doesn't even flinch.

"Long time no see, Mango," Greer says in that way he *thinks* is cavalier, but mostly comes across as slimy.

Harper had a weird fascination with him right before she left. The recollection pops up suddenly, and she peers at Greer, trying to see what it was that had made Harper so *intense* whenever he'd been around. He's cut off the sleeves of his t-shirt, so that the side of his fish-white pecs show, which, if he wasn't a boy, would be pretty sexy, but mostly comes off as narcissistic here in broad daylight. Barbed wire and eagles write black stories down his arms and neck, and his bleached out hair is shaved a lot like Carmen and Haiden's, but shorter on top. His eyes are long and blue, his nose small and straight, and his mouth round and full, which she guesses must have been what Harper was reacting to. He smells of clove cologne—the kind favored by teen boys everywhere and usually parted with by men over the age of 21—and he is too much this afternoon.

There's little to say about Walsh. He's a typical stocky Blackpines boy: dark hair slicked back Mafia-style and strangely thin brows. Pasty at the edges of a farmer's tan. He's quieter, though, and easier to handle in his long silences. He would've made a much more understandable object of affection, but Harper always liked people who defied the low-energy Blackpines stereotype. He never liked seeing himself in anyone else.

She turns her attention to Carmen and Haiden (easier on

the eyes).

"Nothing to say, Maya? See you haven't changed." Greer pauses, lifts his nose, and gives a dramatic sniff. "Well."

Jude stiffens beside her. Not like normal people do—in the shoulders or the face—but more a low-octave vibration. Maya tries elbowing her again, but Jude is deceptively sturdy. Under that dirty white dress, she is as hard as iron. It's like elbowing a stack of grain, and Maya reaches out, catching Jude's skirt between two fingers, as though it'll stop her if she wants to curse anyone in broad daylight.

The silence goes on too long, and Greer looks less cocky and a little more mean—more like the boy she remembers.

"What's your problem?" he growls. "You've been trespassing on our home, and you can't even say fucking hello?"

"That's not the way we work, and you know it," Haiden says, still watching Maya warily—still gripping Carmen's hand. "The only ones not welcome are...*them*."

"Whatever, Haybale. I don't fucking care. Maya here thinks she's too good for us. *That's* the fucking problem."

"Sad creature, we do not need your permission. We do not owe you attention." Jude's voice is low, humming with magic. It purrs like an angry cat, and the crow lets out a squawk, flapping its wings.

"What the fuck is with Wednesday over here?" Greer demands, but he edges away, and Maya smiles with all her teeth.

"Caleb, let's just leave them alone," Carmen says, pulling away from Haiden to grab his elbow. "They aren't hurting anyone."

"No, I want to know what they're doing, snooping around

here. Do you not think that's suspicious as shit?" But he doesn't shrug Carmen off, and he doesn't meet Jude's eyes—not quite—though she stares, unblinking, at him. "We've got your boy—the one you bit. You bit him, right? That's what Harpy says. You don't even want to check on him? What's so important you won't even check on your puppy?"

Jude laughs, and it burns through the dryer-hot air like the first crack of thunder. The crow caws and caws behind her—laughing or screaming, Maya can't tell. "We are not babysitters. We did not come here to take care of little boys."

Maya shakes her head. "We're here on *our* business, Greer. It doesn't affect you in any way, which means it's none of *your* business."

"Fucking bi—"

Carmen smacks him in the back of the head, scowling, and Haiden takes a step forward, looking mutinous.

He glances at them and frowns, but doesn't apologize. He doesn't repeat the insult, either. He clears his throat. "You've always been weird, Maya. Fucking unfriendly. And now you don't even have Harpy to stand behind."

"Do I look like I need someone to hide behind?" she asks, lilting and sweet as she can muster.

"If you decide to stop being a— Whatever. *Whatever.* If you want to see him, we aren't going to run you off. It's an easy turn off the highway. I hope you find what you're looking for and fuck off. C'mon, Angus. Angus?"

But Maya can see that Angus has wandered into the general store, now standing at the counter.

"If you do want to see him," Haiden says, moving to Greer and putting a hand on his shoulder consolingly, "you *are* welcome here. Any wolf who means no harm is welcome in Libra territory, and that includes at the L. If you need food or a shower or whatever. We haven't seen you in a long time."

"Miranda isn't one of us, is she?" Maya asks.

The wolves blink, and then Greer laughs. "Oh, fuck no. She's got three kids in Trenton. She ran off with a used car salesman two weeks before graduation. Man, she was fucking hot. Took her to junior prom, except we never went in. She went down—"

"Will you fuck off, Caleb?" Haiden snaps, giving him a shove. "That's not cool."

"Guess she has that in common with Harpy," he adds a little too forcefully.

It's funny how all their noses wrinkle at the same time. It endears Carmen and Haiden to her, and she considers (briefly) the merits of heading to Knuckle Bones with the two of them and maybe catching up after all. But Greer is still giving her that gross, knowing look, and Maya thinks of crystalline beaches and seagulls and anything except Harper and Greer—

Ugh.

"That's messed up," Carmen mutters. "Talking about people like that, like you don't fucking care who it was, like they didn't matter as people."

"Jesus Christ, Carmen. Stop fucking lecturing me. You may not have noticed, but Harpy and me? We aren't friends. He never passes up a chance to treat me like a fucking STD. I don't owe him—"

"Maybe," Maya finally says, glossing over Greer, replying

straight to Haiden. "We might." She studies Haiden's face, searching for evidence of a trick or a trap or trouble, but Haiden mostly looks hot and tired now. She nods slowly. "Maybe."

Jude turns to her, brow cocked, but the buzzing energy fades, and the crow takes flight, soaring away over the low shops. Angus comes outside, blinking at the sun reflecting off the cars and ignoring the deeper, more complicated emotions still brewing. Maya contemplates whether that's a virtue or a vice. Right now, she's perfectly happy to force all the baggage back under their beds.

"It's not Harper's fault, you know."

She turns, realizing Greer is still talking to her.

"You think I'm a shit for talking about a blowjob? At least I'm not blaming him for the worst thing that ever happened to that stupid motherfucker." Greer turns, nodding at Angus, and they walk back the way they came. Angus hands him a smoke, and their conversation becomes too quiet to follow.

"And there goes Toxic Masculinity: Specimen A," Haiden breathes.

"He definitely wishes Harper would give him the time of day," Carmen agrees, fixing her ponytail and smiling sadly.

"Nah, I think he wants—"

But Jude and Maya don't wait to hear about Harper's would-be love life. They're already climbing into Nova's car, and Carmen and Haiden jump in surprise as the engine turns over.

"Come by... if you want?" Carmen calls, waving as they pull away.

Jude sticks her hand out the window, gestures something

that seems friendly, but in a way Maya is sure no normal person has ever used to say *hello* or *good-bye*. She tucks her pink feet on the dashboard and combs through Nova's mix tapes, popping in something that sounds like a carnival gone wrong—heady, with bursts of guitar and a woman's raspy singing. Better than the sugar-sweet pop stuff, Maya supposes.

They drive silently, following the simple path described beneath rolling clouds and summer-blue skies and through seeding grass and high stalks of corn. It reminds her of driving home after school, sharing gummi bears with Harper, tucked deep into the bus seat, paper flying overhead... Harper and Maya, together in the trenches of the Blackpines school system. But thinking about Harper makes her want to cry, and she feels brittle enough already, strangely unsettled by the altercation.

She knows the L, or she knows of it: the big, private lodge at the edge of the park. She hadn't known who owned it. She'd always assumed it was someone too rich and snobby to invite local kids over. But she knows where it is. Her stomach clenches as they turn off the highway, and she pulls halfway onto the shoulder. The sunlight has gone from white to orange to a bright cadmium red, glowing through the gaps between oak leaves and sweeping in a dappled blanket over the front seat of the car, across their arms and legs.

Jude is still for a long moment, and then her hand goes to Maya's knee. She studies Maya's face like she's checking for injury. Maya nods and puts her hand over Jude's knuckles.

"Do you love him? The one you bit?" Jude asks.

Maya sighs, trying to gently shoo a bee away from the driver's side window.

"You went after him. You could have been bitten. It was foolish. Very foolish."

"Would you have left if I had been?"

Jude doesn't reply, and Maya takes it for the honesty it is. She's about to say that's fair when Jude asks, "Would you? If it was me?"

Maya turns to her, and Jude looks fragile, washed out and sickly, curled in the passenger seat. She's too organic. Too—

"I wouldn't want to," she says, carefully.

Jude nods solemnly. "I wouldn't want to either."

She blinks in surprise. Jude smiles at her and then sits up, pulls away, and digs under the seat for a bottle of water. She takes a long drink and hands it to Maya. The lip tastes a little like coffee.

"I can't," Maya says, sighing into the bottle until it whistles angrily. "I can't see him. Them. It was so hard to leave them the first time..." But she had, because *Lucía*. She could give up almost anything for Lucía, go through nearly any sadness or pain, but only for Lucía, and even then, losing them hurt for a long, long time.

She takes the keys from the ignition, tucking them into the glove compartment.

"So we leave it here," Jude says, turning to gather her stuff from the back.

"Is there anyone you miss? Anyone you can't see anymore?" Maya asks.

"Just Mamaw," Jude replies, kicking open the door and hopping out. "I'm not lonely, though. Not like you. Not with you."

Maya climbs out, leaning on the hood with her forearms, not sure what to make of that, but Jude has her back to the car. She sighs, ducking back inside to grab her bag, and pulls out a scrunchie to pile her hair into a bun atop her head.

Nova is nearby. She tries not to think about it, but the knowing is here, pressing against her skin, beckoning her. Nova is so close, and she *does* love him. She wants to see that he is safe, to confirm it for herself. Her chest feels strange, and she rubs it, trying to unearth sadness from between her bones, but it stays stuck.

Nova is okay, though. He's safe where he is. She got him to the people who can take care of him. That's all she can do for him right now.

Right now, he's not the one in trouble.

Right now—

She slams the door and heads into the thick pines, past a forgotten camper, and away from Nova and Harper and further distraction.

vii. nova

(every time you breathe in,
a little of the universe gets stuck in your lungs,
every time you exhale, you lose more of yourself)

They tried putting the dogs in the bed of the truck, but Whale whined and kept trying to squeeze through the slit in the back window until Harper had to pull over so Nova could bring him inside, and when Whale was in the cab, Abbott and Costello decided that it was dreadfully unfair that they be left in the bed of the truck—Abbott sticking his nose through the window and mournfully whuffling the side of Nova's neck, Costello howling into the rushing wind as though the world had come to its end. So they had to pull over again and let all the dogs into the cab. Nova supposes it's a funny picture: him and three dogs crammed onto the tiny backseat, Whale with his head on Nova's thigh, Costello flopped beside his other leg, and Abbott sitting up straight, drinking in the wind from Harper's window.

Putting Mason in the passenger's seat had felt intuitive—like parents arranging siblings in anticipation of afternoon tantrums. It would have been weird to have Mason sitting behind him, feeling left out and frustrated, and staring holes into the top of his head. Or maybe it was a different instinct. Because more than uncomfortable, it would've been agonizing to be pinned between Harper and Mason. He might have suffocated to death. As it is, Harper keeps stealing glances in the rear view, and Mason only stops looking at him from the mirror on the shade when their eyes meet, and he realizes Nova has noticed.

It's too hot for this, he thinks, rubbing his face on his shoulder and plucking at his shirt. He doesn't know whose clothing he's wearing, but the shirt is too long and tighter than he likes in the chest and shoulders. It looks like a supermarket t-shirt, the kind that comes three in a bag. The jeans are also too big, rolled at the ankle over drug store flip flops that pinch his hot feet. He hopes his car will be easy to find, and they won't have to do much walking. His feet might fall off.

But he is fed and clean, and that's better than things have been.

"We have that going for us," he tells Whale, scratching his hips.

"What's that?" Harper asks, looking at him again.

He thinks better of telling Harper that he's talking to the dog and, as Mason surely knows, avoiding everyone else. He swallows.

They're really looking at him now, on and off, on and off, over and over and over—and their blue eyes are completely different and yet eerily similar. He wishes they'd follow his lead and pretend he isn't here, or that one of them might have the decency to kick the elephant in the room in its pachyderm ass and get this over with.

A childish voice suggests kicking the seat as a way to instigate conversation, but that feels unnecessarily violent after a week of unnecessary violence, and he's grown out of kicking things when frustrated. It never worked with his moms anyway, never made them see his side over Saturno's, and mostly landed him in trouble. He doubts it would be any different here. He digs his fingers into Whale's fur and scratches deeper, and Whale sighs in utter bliss.

Useful exorcisms of unwanted energy.

"Say it," he says, trying to keep his voice flat, but there's a hummingbird of pure German *angst* buzzing in the syllables. "Don't play stupid. Just say what you want to say."

"Fine." Mason stops looking at him, sits deeper in his seat and crosses his arms tightly in front of him, so that only his elbows are visible from the back. "You left without saying anything, and then you continued to not say anything to the point that people *kidnapped* you, and I only knew because Harper figured it out."

"I didn't figure it out," Harper mumbles. "Maya warned me. I wouldn't have realized it either, not without her."

"So basically without Maya, you'd be fucked," Mason says, and Harper nods.

"Well, that's just par for the course."

He ruffles Whale's ears and weighs how stupid it would be to point out that he never expected, assumed, or imagined anyone coming to his rescue—and he *almost* escaped on his own. Almost. Besides which, it was Libra's arrival that turned the tide. But all of that would be unkind when he knows that Harper and Mason bent over backwards to rescue him. There's still too much worry haunting their faces. Still too much love.

"Are you going to explain anything? Why you left? Why you stopped talking to me? What did I do that was so terrible? What were you even doing in L.A.?"

Mason sits up, and Nova tries to shrink into the half-door.

"And me. Me, too," Harper adds. He's gone very quiet, the way he always does when he's exposed something personal and fears the immediate repercussions of his vulnerability. Nova had hoped he would have grown past that and stopped expecting pain as the inevitable result of opening himself to the world.

His guts twist.

Luckily I have two sets of intestines. Harper can tangle the small, and Mason can knot the large!

He bites his lip to keep from laughing, because he feels a little hysterical, and hysterical laughter has only ever upset Mason more. If he freaks out in front of Harper, Harper might bury himself so deep in these woods, the locals will start mistaking him for Bigfoot.

"Okay, okay. Let me think." He pulls Whale fully into his lap, slouching behind Mason's seat to escape the reflections of their eyes. "First, let me make sure I understand the charges. I ran out on you, Harper Lovell, three years ago. I think it was May, right? Yeah, May. Aggravated abandonment, because I never explained. Parole also didn't go well, because I never checked in. Then I left you, Mason Murray, one and a half years ago—two months before your birthday, as I recall. Again, aggravated charges, due to lack of explanation and, in the parole period, contact. That's how you want me to say it, right? Multiple accounts of aggravated asshattery."

"Please don't," Mason groans, turning towards him, but Nova ducks against the door again. Harper remains silent, uneasy and probably hurt, just as expected. Well, at least it didn't catch him off-guard.

Nova considers beating his head against the glass.

"I'm taking everything seriously, Mason. That's the problem. You don't believe I take anything seriously, and I always take everything seriously. I have been taking things seriously from day one. I'm only confessing to my criminal history because I know it's true."

"I can't do this," Harper mumbles. There's desperation in his hands as they cross the wheel and veer the truck into an abandoned gas station.

Outside, the concrete glitters with broken glass, the window front lined with browning cracks. Hoses trail from their pumps, snaking into the lanes, and tickers leer back at them, burned orange with age and sunlight. Nova considers forcing his body through the back window and escaping. He could make a new life here. There might be bags of cotton candy and pretzels. Those things never go bad. Though a life lived on stale pretzels seems like a pretty steep sentence for crimes of the heart.

He laughs this time.

Mason cringes, and Harper hits the brakes, sending them all jerking forward. It knocks the laughter from his lungs, and Nova sits back, trapped between the window and their confusion. He stares at the back of their heads.

The past is always between me and freedom.

Shit.

He runs his hands over his face. "I'm sorry. Okay? I'm sorry. Please continue to drive. The ghosts of those unwanted pretzels are staring at me, and I can't take their judgment, too. I've already got yours and yours and mine to deal with."

"I'm not... I don't want to punish you," Harper whispers. He looks away from Nova and Mason—perhaps searching for pretzel ghosts. "Maybe I thought about it. I mean, anyone would have. But I don't... That's *not* what I want. I just want to understand."

"That's not what I want *either,*" Mason says, sounding wobbly. "Look, I was angry—*am* angry. But you aren't just my ex, you're supposed to be my *best friend.* We've been friends for almost 20 years, but you couldn't even say why you were leaving—"

"You know why I left!" Nova shouts, knocking Whale from his lap, and jamming his finger into the air between Mason and Harper.

"No, I *don't!*" Mason shouts back.

"I make you fucking unhappy!" he replies in a pretty decent bellow.

Frustration wells in his throat, trying to bubble over, but there's nowhere for it to go—not with him cornered and in the wrong, not unless he wants to really make an asshole of himself, and he knows he does not. He throws himself back into his seat and smacks his head on the window. Prodding it with his fingers, he studies the felted roof of the cab. It's oddly spotless, and he wonders if Harper actually takes the time to clean it. Closing his eyes, he releases a long sigh, pressing his head against the back window until it hurts to let the discomfort ground him.

"I made you miserable," he repeats, lowering his voice. "I made you unhappy, and it made me even more fucked up. I couldn't do it anymore. I couldn't do it to you, and I couldn't do it to me. I thought you understood."

Mason doesn't reply. His hand, Nova notes from the crack between seat and door, is clenched on the handle, but he doesn't move. Nova tries to find his face in the mirror, but he's the one ducking now, and Nova can only guess at how upset he is and over which particulars. He blows his hair from his eyes and tries Harper, also rooted in place, arms locked and fingers tight around the wheel. He stares ahead fixedly, and Nova thinks he might be holding his breath, waiting for the other shoe to fall on his head and concuss him permanently this time.

He puts his face in his hands. He has to be more delicate, less like he's reading from a script that's played out a thousand times. He tries again.

"Maya left, yes. But that's not why I left. That's not the reason at all."

It's easier with Harper. They never really fought, never fell into that rut. It's easier and harder, too, because there's also no blueprint to Harper's hurt and anger. Mason won't get out of the car if he hasn't already fled. He's going to stew—to think of something biting and brutal to say. Not because he's cruel, though it is a decidedly cruel outcome, but because sometimes the only way Mason can express how badly he's hurting is by replying with unkindness equivalent to the pain he feels. And it would be too easy if he just said,

That's enough, Nova.

That's what happens when you grow up together: you grow fluent in that person's logic, accustomed to their impaired communication patterns, and it's all too easy to subscribe to those familiar patterns, to forget that he can-could-*should* have said, *That's not fair.*

That you could have said it, too.

Because it *seems* like that kind of closeness would be ideal. You can intuit where they're coming from. You know how they feel without words. Being a *we* starts to feel effortless, but effortless is bad. Effortless means you stop trying in all the places you need to try hardest.

And, at the same time, knowing someone so well, you become immersed. Little patterns begin to form, starting with inside jokes and nicknames, becoming the shapes of confessions and fights alike, and then those quirks are just how you communicate—they become their own language, like the babbling conversations between baby twins. You forget objectivity, forget to say stop, and you lose track of when you're supposed to hit the brakes on a corrupted communication system.

You look back, and it's a burning pile filled with words no one ever meant, engulfing the feelings you did.

Did.

Do.

Done.

Harper, though...Harper is an unknown quantity, and Nova lets Whale back into his lap, stroking him from head to tail in apology. He allows himself another sigh before he continues.

"I didn't know what you wanted. When Maya was around, it seemed simple. We were just passing time, right? Just hooking up or whatever. But when it was the two of us, it felt like things either needed to become something, or we should call it quits. I don't know. Did I read it wrong? You didn't seem like you were going to ask me to stay, and I thought if I just... If I didn't leave... I'm sorry. I got scared. I *did* want to be with you, and I was scared of what that meant when I also had feelings for Mason, and you seemed ambivalent about making us an *us*. All these things were ending at the same time. I thought it would make more sense if I just left, before the window shut on my fingers. I didn't think it'd shut on yours."

Harper looks like someone's hit him in the face—blinking slowly, turning pink. Silent.

Mason stays silent as well, sitting back slowly and letting his breath empty in a thin stream until the life has gone out of him. Nova can sense the heft of his body against the seat. He wants to reach out and touch Mason. They made the most sense when it was reassuring touches at the right moment, uncomplicated and real, anchoring and kind. But he can't both damage Mason and console him. That feels like a choice bound for somewhere dark.

Look, Ma! Boundaries!

He watches the silhouettes of weeds tapping the dirty windows beyond the pumps.

"All I do is hurt you, Mason, and honestly... If I *had* stayed, I would probably have hurt you even worse, Harper. That's just what I do. I'm a figurative supernova, and the only thing I create is bright, burning disasters."

"Do you actually mean that, or are you being dramatic?" Harper asks, still fixed on the steering wheel.

"*Or* is this some roundabout plea for sympathy?" Mason asks, voice flat and brittle.

"I guess I mean it." Nova shrugs, kicking off his flip flops and putting his feet on the back of Mason's seat. He tucks his knees, so that Whale is sheltered between thigh and stomach. This is the safest world: just him and Whale, who he can't hurt, who he can't fuck up, who loves him in a clean and easy way. This is how things should be with them, too, but that's never been more than wishful thinking.

His eyes wander over the dogs, taking in their states of boredom (Costello) and anxiety (Abbott and Whale), and after a moment, he muses aloud, "Sometimes I think about what it would be like if we loved each other the same way we do when we're wolves. Maybe if we could, we'd be happy. But even that's an illusion, isn't it? Even that's not simple."

Harper cuts in, his voice soft, "I had a lot of time to think after you went home." His head rolls across the headrest to follow Nova's gaze to the store. Nova wonders if he's also watching the dance of the weeds, or if he's looking for shapes in the clouds of dirt hanging on the glass. He stretches one arm out the window, turning his gaze to the tips of his fingers, and reaches for something unseen. "I wanted to ask you to stay, but I didn't, because I thought you wanted to go home to..." He doesn't look at Mason, but it feels like he does. Mason tries to hug himself into something tiny, and Nova tries not to notice.

"If you wanted to be with him, there wasn't a point in asking you to stay. I just wished it could be a little longer, mean a little more, or... I don't know. I didn't know if it meant something—anything—to *you*... It pissed me off. You were just one more person who disappeared. One more missed chance. I wanted to hate you. I wanted to tell you to fuck off into the sun. But now I'm not sure what I want to say. Just that it sucked. It sucked a lot. It still sucks. But you're hard to hate, so you know... I don't hate you. Whatever, I guess."

Mason laughs dryly. It sounds like a cough. But he doesn't remark, which Nova thinks is nice of him. Nova can see him staring into the fragments of his own reflection. Always looking inward, never finding.

"When it all comes down to it, I still feel the way I felt," Nova says after a moment. "But I am *not okay*, and that's kind of a problem. I'm telling myself it's not an insurmountable hurdle, but after a zillion mirror-front pep talks, it hasn't stuck. Still, it *did* mean something. To me."

This would make more sense one-on-one, but there's a part of him that's relieved to say it all at once. The end result is the same: nothing can come of their confessions. There's empirical proof that he has hurt them and does not know how to avoid doing it again. It all comes back to patterns, and he hasn't broken his. They're still living in the disaster area burying his heart. So maybe it is better to get it over with in one fell swoop. He just wishes that swoop would fell him a little faster.

"You *didn't* make me unhappy," Mason murmurs, arms locked around his ribs. "Back then, I didn't say what I was thinking, and I thought, you know, that we had this unspoken connection, so when you didn't get what I needed, it felt like a slap in the face. But that wasn't fair."

"Seriously," Harper mutters, and Mason shoots him a look.

Nova tries not to laugh, rubbing his cheek on his shoulder.

"I couldn't understand..." Mason continues, tripping over his own hesitation. He clears his throat. "If you loved me as much as I loved you, how could you give up on us? I guess...I was being naive." He can see Mason biting his lip in the overhead mirror. He can see the unshed gleam in his eyes and the swallow that pushes it down again. "But I don't understand what you mean. You've always been so...*you*. How not okay is 'not okay'? What exactly is 'not okay'? Is it because of me? Because of us?"

Harper stays silent, but the sudden set of his jaw suggests he's worried about the same thing. Nova exhales slowly, pushing his hair out of his face and looking out the window.

"Can we please drive? It's a long story, and this place is depressing as hell, so unless we're going to break in and liberate some cigarettes from the weeds..."

"Yeah. Okay, sure," Harper says, starting the truck back up. Costello barks, nose pressed to the back window, his nub of a tail jumping back and forth. Nova leans against the door, resting his ankles on the border collie, and thinks about where to begin.

"It starts around Christmas. That's the catalyst, but it doesn't all unfold then. So some of this won't make sense until later. But here's what happened: Saturno brought his girlfriend home. I'd met her a couple of times before, but I guess for him, this was a kind of *coup de grace*. You see, he brought her home to announce their engagement. Basically, he wanted to make his victory very clear."

His mind skirts over the image, flinching at the touch. It's still such a tender memory. Even coming close to it makes him want to curl up and hide forever—

The smallest suggestion of a belly at the hem of the ugly sweater, an arm stretched around the shoulders of a matching green atrocity. His brother's teeth bared to the Christmas lights, mouth pulled into a lazy smile, and Emily tucking a curl of brown hair behind one ear, her smile toothless. Red light blinking in a gold band, and Mama's happy shout...

Nova fades into the background, becomes part of the couch, a flat smile frozen on his face, a robotic nod moving his head up and down. His brother's cold eyes, darker than his own, hold his gaze, preventing him from escaping into the background, demanding that he acknowledge defeat. Saturno's happy smile twists, becomes sharp and canny and cruel.

Nova shivers and shakes his head, drags himself back into the present.

"In the far corner, we have Saturno, newly engaged to a fresh-faced, lovely human being. Lovely, like she always gets up to help clear the dishes and compliments the house and shares funny stories about someone named Saturno, who I have never met, because according to her, he sounds like a great guy. Yes, here we have Saturno, successful in romance and business—in life, as we are told it matters. And in the other corner, we have me, fresh out of two failed relationships, with a theatre degree that's gone nowhere, and who has, as you will recall, returned to residency in the attic of his childhood home for some months. A fucking fantastic disappointment in the flesh."

Mason makes a soft noise—the kind that precedes a, *That's not true!*—but Nova continues before he can get it out. "So! We have super shiny Saturno, king of his world, and fucking loser Nova, who has wrecked everything he has ever touched, and the two are enjoying a touching Christmas dinner with the soon-to-be Mrs. Emily Vasco."

He scratches his freshly-shaven chin, watching clouds growing heavy and bruised in the opposite window and laughs thinly. "It's funny how exhausting life becomes when you're doing nothing for a prolonged period of time. I know neither of you can understand, as you're both productive all the time—at work and play—but anyway, I suppose you could call it a Depression, or just depression. I wasn't shiny or fun, but I was, you know, a basic level of decent and, more often than not, aspiring to gregariousness, warmth, and helpfulness in Emily's presence. I didn't remember her hating me the last time we talked, but she clearly found me objectionable this time around.

"I tried to make good with her, or at least to stay out of their way, but inevitably Saturno and I got into it. There was the usual aperitif: roundabout insults aimed at my personal integrity. I mean, you'd think he would've given up on the whole subliminal message thing at 12—my moms didn't throw me out then, and they weren't going to now—but he couldn't get through dinner without starting something, and I was fucking tired, the way you are when nothing looks up and everything feels empty. I was tired, and he started *name dropping*, and I got pissed. We started yelling at each other across the table, and then everyone was upset. Mama was shouting at both of us, Mom was trying to calm everyone down, and Emily was just staring at me, shaking her head.

"Fast forward to later that night: I go downstairs to piss somewhere around midnight, and I can hear them talking. I think to myself, *Don't.* But sometimes you just...do anyway. I put my ear to the door, and I can hear her saying shit like, *Yeah, no kidding. He's just like you said.* And then he goes on this dead-horse rant about how I'm a waste of space, so I continue on my way. After that, nothing happened. Christmas went on as planned, and Emily and Saturno drove home. Peace was restored to the lands. But I couldn't stop thinking about it. All this shit he claimed I'd done, all these personality traits he'd invented for me—most of it was shit *he* had done to *me.* Like that fight at dinner: *he* fucking picked it, but then he twisted the story, and it's suddenly because I was talking over him, or looking down on him. He tells her how I'm trying to make him look bad, how I'm everyone's favorite, and how I use that against him. He twists and twists and twists...

"And it's fucking hypocritical. It's fucking unfair. I know it's messed up. So why can't I stop thinking about it? And then I start thinking that maybe I'm wrong. How can we be telling the exact same story about the other person and *both* be in the right? One of us lacks self-awareness. One of us is in deep denial. Clearly one brother *is* going out of his way to make life bad for the other. At some point—usually just before the birds wake up—you start to question if you aren't the bad guy after all. So I start filling notebooks. I write down fights and incidents that stick out in my head. Some of them didn't happen at home, but for those that did, I'd ask Mama if she could remember. Only, she would gloss over it, say it was boys being boys—that kind of thing. I'd ask Mom, too, but she had been at work for a lot of the incidents, and she didn't remember much.

"So I think: *Are they just sparing my feelings?* I'd always felt like they were protecting *him* with that noncommittal shit, but the more I thought about it, the more I started to second-guess every interaction I'd ever had with him. Sometimes, I'd pick up the phone, and I'd start to text you, Mason—to see if you remembered it the way I did. But I didn't want to call you at 2 A.M. I didn't think you wanted to talk to me. I was a *persona non grata*, and I didn't feel like I belonged in your life.

"So I ruined that notebook. I wrote all these arguments in the margins, around my lists and recollections. Layers and layers of self-defense, written over and then written over again with more doubts. One day I was highlighting some stuff, and I thought, *This isn't healthy.* I knew some-thing was wrong with me. I did some quizzes online, but they only made me more paranoid. I thought I was going through some big dissociative...*thing*, and if it was— But I had to fucking know for sure. I'm sorry, Mason. I went to your dad's house, and I asked him if I could look around. He didn't ask questions. He gave me chamomile tea and let me into your room, and I found your spiral bounds in the box under your bed."

"What the fuck? *You read my journals?*"

"I'm sorry. I didn't...I didn't know where else to turn. I had to know if I was having a break with reality. I had to.

You don't understand. *I had to.*"

"Or what?"

"Pass."

"*Nova.*"

Harper slows, eyes flicking to the rearview, the furrow in his brow deep. Mason turns to look at him over the back of the seat, and Nova crosses his arms, refusing to meet his gaze.

"I only read the parts about me and Saturno. They lined up with my memories. But see, doubting myself that long? Being fucked up all the time for months? It felt like I had all these lesions inside me. Instead of feeling better, I continued to feel jumpy and guilty and bad. Just...bad. When someone goes after you like that, when it's so targeted and prolonged... You can know, on some level, that it's not because you actually did something wrong, but because you didn't do what they wanted you to. You can know it, but if you spend enough time alone with that, it shakes your confidence. It makes it that much harder to believe there's anything good about you.

"Saturno has been trying to convince people to hate me since we were kids. His buddies didn't hit me just because I was small, and Emily didn't start to dislike me over a single argument. Maybe his friends were fuckwits, but she's a normal, sensible person. That means something. I got really paranoid about being home. I felt like my moms were going to start thinking that he was right about me. I was scared they would hate me if I stayed. I had to somehow prove he was wrong, so one day, I did what I do best: I packed a bag, wrote a note promising to call, and started driving."

Mason sighs, unfolding and rubbing his eyes. Harper returns his attention to the road, peering at the thunderheads in the rearview. And for the moment, Nova is relieved of their attention. He lets out a soft, secret sigh and pinches the space between his brows.

"We should head back. This is going to be a big one," Harper says, still leaning forward.

"I don't want to go back to the L right now. How far away is your place?" Nova asks.

Harper opens his mouth—surprised, or maybe hesitant—and Nova is about to say, *Nevermind*, when he shrugs.

"Not far."

"Is it okay if we go there?"

Harper nods, pulling onto a dirt road to turn around.

"Thanks."

"Yeah, no problem," he says, but he's tense, and Nova can *feel* it resonating, echoing, in his own shoulders. He glances at Mason, who has his eyes closed, face turned towards the window—breathing evenly, but too rigid to be asleep. He rubs his wrist and wishes he knew what to say. Happily, Harper turns on the radio, and he is released from the swell of silence. Nova slowly exhales, glad to stop talking (to stop remembering), and focuses on the clouds pooling ahead of them.

"So that was what it was? Trying to find yourself?" Mason suddenly asks, eyes still shut.

"I don't know. Close enough, probably."

"But you're still not okay."

"Not really."

There's a moment of quiet before Mason asks, "What does

that mean for us?"

Nova laughs, watching the first vines of lightning thread across the sky.

"I don't know."

viii. harper

(turn your eyes away from the stars,
those uv rays will burn out the retinas;
looking truth in the face will make you go blind)

"Porfa?"

Nova holds out the scissors, and Harper can see the dark smudge of his reflection looping around their handle. He has no eyes. He has only the saddest of tans. It's all dark hair and the vague, peach-pale impression of his skin. He slips them from Nova's fingers, wondering where he found them, but doesn't ask. He sits Nova in the living room, on his only stool.

"Why didn't you ask me?" Mason says from the couch, a beer in one hand, his phone in the other. Beside him, Costello stretches across the rest of the cushions, having temporarily given up on knocking the beer from Mason's hand.

"You're good at a lot of things, but you are not good with hair," Nova replies, bouncing on the stool and scraping his fingers through his hair.

"I have a comb," Harper says, feeling a little shy. He

avoids Mason's eyes and takes a curling, sable lock in hand. He's glad he untangled most of it while Nova was asleep. It sits soft and smooth against his palm, easy to snip.

He'd let Nova cut his hair, back in university. It had looked about the same back then, but Nova managed to give it some shape—convinced him briefly to shave it over one ear, to try to coax it over the top of his head into something modern, but he'd given up on styling it early on, and then it grew out entirely. Nova had always been particular about his hair. He'd always done it himself, jumping between a straight razor and an electric one until it was the *right* shape. Harper had rarely understood what that meant, but he'd always been impressed. He doesn't know why Nova wants him to cut it now, but he thinks it probably harkens back to that 'Depression or depression' thing, and he's always liked it when Aunt Jelly trimmed his hair for him. It always made him feel taken care of, maybe even safe.

"What do you want me to do with it?" he asks, stroking the seal-slick piece. Rain beats loud and dense on the windows. Thunder booms from afar—not close enough to spook Abbott, just a suggestion of bass from many miles away.

"Medium and shaggy. Like it was last summer."

"Do you have a picture?"

"Yeah, I—" Nova reaches for his hip and stops, sighing. "My phone is in my car."

Curiously, Mason doesn't offer to look it up. Harper glances at him, watching him take long drinks from the can, running his teeth over his lower lip to catch the drops. His mouth grows fuller and redder the more he drinks, and he looks up before Harper can look away.

Fuck me.

"That's okay. I can look," he quickly mutters and pulls out his phone, staring at it pointedly for a moment before unlocking it. His notifications are flooded with messages from his uncles. He marks them all as read and pulls up Nova's social. Mason turns up the T.V., but it's still too quiet—an impression of a baseball game, softer than the dogs' snores. He finds a couple of pictures, swiping back and forth between them, and stuffs the phone back into his pocket. Mason peers at the television, brow pinched. He seems confused by what he's watching.

"I played baseball in high school," Harper says, closing the blades on the first lock of hair and only cringing a little.

Mason looks up, looks surprised—doesn't look at Nova. He turns to Harper like it's natural to look at Harper and not Nova when he's sitting between them, and Harper wonders if that means something, or if he's the only one magnetized by Nova, and Mason is just exercising social skills like a regular, well-rounded human being. He clears his throat and resumes snipping.

"My dad used to play catch with me, but we weren't really the type. We'd get bored and start talking about books, about the girl he almost married in Japan, about... Well, stuff like that. Eventually we'd be so deep in conversation that the ball would roll off and disappear. He'd have to buy a new one for the next time."

Mason laughs, and his face opens unexpectedly—pink clouds beneath constellations of freckles, floating brightly over a braces-straight kind of smile. Harper can see Mason at 13 or 14 with a mouth full of metal—too awkward to step outside the house, except for Nova. Nova would have made it easier. Nova would have made it good. He'd made it good for Harper, made each day exciting, shooed away Harper's anxieties with pleasant anticipation.

Nova looks at him, eyes wide—uncertain or surprised or something harder to place in the shallow angle of his face. Harper shrugs and continues shaping.

"My uncle was a baseball star back in the day. But he fucked up his knee in university and wound up dropping out of school. He taught me to play. I guess that was his way of being a dad without trying to be my dad."

Nova squeezes the seams of his jeans, puckering the muscles atop his thighs. Harper wonders what it is: growing up without a dad, or the trust that's tentatively sprouted between him and Mason. Mason doesn't look like he's sure what to do with that either. He gets up and takes another beer without asking, and the house briefly feels as domestic and cozy as the apartment back in college.

Harper nearly trims the tip of his middle finger, jerking away just as metal starts to pinch skin.

Wake up.

Shaking his head, he runs his fingers through Nova's hair, trying to figure out which section to attack next—trying not to enjoy it too much. Nova sighs, folding into his touch, and Harper thinks, for a moment, about how good it could be if things were always like this: the three of them, comfortable in their familiarity, breathing side by side.

Like a pack.

But he already knows it isn't a pack he's thinking of, and

what he wants is not possible—not with Nova being where he is now, not after that conversation in the truck.

"You could have called," he suddenly says. "I would have answered. It wouldn't— You wouldn't have been bothering me. I'm sorry you didn't think you could."

Nova straightens, and Harper thinks he must have opened his eyes, because Mason seems to be trying to chase his expression, and Nova seems to be deftly slipping free of his gaze, turning just a little—away from them both.

"I'm sorry I didn't call," Harper continues, cutting the curl—fully realized—over his right ear. "I didn't want to overstep. I didn't—" He purses his mouth, trying to make the words come: *I was insecure. I was hurt. I didn't know if I had a place in your life. I didn't want you to hurt me again. I didn't want you to hate me. I wanted to hate you.* But they stay clogged beneath his clavicle, dragged by their own weight back into all the unsaid things that live in his chest. Gone again. "I wish I had called. I'm sorry."

"I should have called," Mason says, turned sideways on the couch and watching sheets of water roll down the glass. "I sensed something was up. I knew you'd gone silent. I just didn't— I misread it. I thought you'd met someone new, that you were making friends, that you were busy. L.A. seems like the kind of place you'd get lost in. I thought you were probably happy there. I was too obsessed with how alone I felt. I didn't think about whether you were alone, too."

"I was busy once I got to L.A." Nova sighs. "Every weekend, I was in some rich fuck's backyard making balloon animals for kids whose allowance was more than my food budget, and every night, I was perfecting the worst pirate accent you can imagine at that shithole restaurant. I spent mornings and most lunches with about fifty yappy dogs strapped to my arms, or lugging groceries up palatial driveaways. I was a slave to the rich." Nova shakes his head, and Harper barely avoids cutting off a big chunk of hair. He gives a warning tug, and Nova offers him a tired, almost cheeky smile.

"I *was* busy. Once I left home, I stayed busy enough to remain functioning. I just wasn't, you know, sunbathing all afternoon in Malibu, or dancing the night away in West Hollywood. Just thinking about dancing after five hours at the restaurant..."

"Don't shake your head."

"Sorry, sorry. But I was mostly okay."

"But you didn't even— You didn't have an apartment," Mason says, softer this time, shoulders rising towards his ears, fingers picking at the white parts of his nails.

"It felt like too much effort. A lot of things felt like too much effort. I pared down, did only what I had to to stay afloat. You don't really need a room if you have a car. You don't really need a shower when there's cheap motels your car can take you to. You don't need friends when you're spending ninety percent of your waking hours working. I existed. I had the stars and enough battery on my phone to listen to music—and I had Whale. It wasn't ideal, but it felt like enough most of the time. I wrung myself out as much as I could, and I didn't have to worry about being a person."

"Cheery."

Nova laughs, a thin, worn down expression of air.

"There's a word for it," Mason says, downing the second beer. "It's called gaslighting. That's what Saturno was doing, making you second-guess everything. All that toxic bullshit... He can't own it, and he probably never will. It works out for him if you blame yourself. But fuck him, none of that was you. I was there. I know. It was him. I was there, but... But I wasn't there when you needed to hear it. I guess it's too late for that to mean anything now."

"No, it's...it's still good to hear. It's good."

"People are fucking...something," Harper says, resting his hands on Nova's ears and turning his head this way and that to survey the job. "I don't get it."

"Well, people are weird. Sometimes weird is good, and sometimes it's bad," Nova replies, trying to sound easy, but there's a jagged exhaustion bleeding into his voice now. Harper runs his fingertips through his hair again, and Nova closes his eyes and lets the façade down for a moment. "I don't know why he does it. I don't think he'll tell me, so I guess I never will understand. It doesn't matter."

Liar.

But Harper doesn't say that either. He runs his fingers up the nape of Nova's neck until he shivers, and after a moment of careful consideration, after a moment of bolstering his guts (for this is the kind of honesty that requires guts), he replies, "*Some* people are weird. Other people are just fuckjacks. You are weird, your brother is an asshole. Don't excuse his bullshit with 'weird.'" He glances at Mason, who nods a little too seriously—face pink, eyes fuzzy.

"Okay."

But Nova is hard under his hands, energy shifting from biting static to impenetrable.

"What is it?" he asks. "What?"

Nova shrugs, and Harper knows what comes next. Laughter, probably (tense and brittle); a joke (half-flat before it's even finished); or maybe a question to throw them off, so they stop asking (so they stop caring).

"What?" he asks again, quieter this time.

"I don't know. I don't, you know? Just— I don't know. Is he a bad person, or is he just messed up—the same as me, but a different shape? I just...don't know. I don't know what I want to say. I don't know."

"Even if he is messed up, that doesn't mean he gets to use you as his personal punching bag. He's just doing it because it's easy," Mason says from the couch, trying to push himself upright, but his spine falls prey to alcohol and gravity. Costello eyes the can slyly.

Nova shrinks, drawing away from him, from them. Heat radiates from the back of his shirt. "I don't know why I'm like this. I don't know why I can't just— I don't know how I feel half the fucking time. I don't know what I'm supposed to do, I don't know how to say what I want to say, and I don't know what I want to say in the first place. There's just too much shit. Seriously... *Seriously!* I feel like my head is a trash compactor full of junky, shit emotion. I try to smash it all down, so that the rest of me can fit. I try to smash it down until it's small enough that I don't notice that it's there. But it feels like it's always just about to overflow, and when it does, it's going to bury me, and it's going to bury you. I'm scared for it to come out. I'm scared that when it does..."

Harper runs his thumbs over the hard bone behind Nova's ears, staring down at his head, trying to translate the jumble of Frantic Nova into something he can understand, something he can respond to. Mason frowns into his can, popping the tab softly.

∘ ∘ ∘

Have you ever been in love?

He'd loved Maya, but he didn't think he was *in love*. It was infatuation, the very definition. Harper shook his head and doggedly sliced peppers, separating the white skeins from the red flesh, flicking away seeds.

Have you?

Maya wasn't home. She'd gone to her dad's for the weekend to watch her stepsiblings. She'd appeared in the hallway with a backpack and a last minute, *See you Monday!*, and that was all the warning they got.

He'd thought it would be hard, just him and Nova skulking about. He thought it would be like babysitting—Nova following him, asking a hundred thousand questions about being a wolf (each question tripping over the previous, fired off before Harper could get a word in). But Nova had mostly kept to himself, equally unsure of how to be alone together. He'd moved with an itch—agitated and quick, leaving when Harper was coming, fidgeting with thin air when there was nowhere else to escape to. He'd crackled—a fistful of wires popping and sparking, their current surging with nowhere to go... Until Sunday night, when Harper had asked what Nova wanted to eat. Until now: Nova chopping onions on a plastic plate and bringing up *love*.

But Nova didn't answer when Harper turned the question around. He put the knife aside and laid his hands flat on the counter, and his shoulders fell as his breath rushed out. His head followed, hair dangling over the white rings of vegetable, and Harper finally understood the tension between them. He pushed Nova against the counter, searching his face, and Nova had cupped his ears and kissed him hard. One of Nova's teeth caught on his lip, and he tasted blood, but he kept kissing Nova, pressing into him, and Nova's fingers dug into the grooves between his spine, leaving half-moon bruises. They stole the air from each other's lungs, passing it back and forth until it was void of oxygen, and Harper's head started spinning.

Sorry.

Nova's teeth grazed his throat, and he forgot to wonder why sorry was the word Nova used. He hadn't recognized Nova's obtuse, brittle side until weeks later, when he'd realized that it was when Nova was snapping and unsettled and difficult that he made the most sense. It was when the façade got too heavy and came tumbling down, when he could see Nova struggling, wrapped up and tangled in that space between illusion and darkness, that he felt he truly understood Nova, and it was easy to love Nova in those moments. It was then that he felt that someone in this world saw him and knew him, too.

∘ ∘ ∘

"It's okay," he says. His hand flattens between Nova's shoulder blades. Nova's heart flexes through his ribs, beating across Harper's palm. He seems small and fragile, the life within him precarious. Harper keeps his hand steady. "If everything comes out, it comes out. You're the good parts and the bad parts. I never hated either. I won't start now."

The muscle under Harper's hand softens, the weight on his wrist deepens. Nova doesn't reply, but he thinks that for once his sorry offering of words have found their mark.

"Someone's here." Mason pushes himself to one knee, twisting over the back of the couch, and squinting against the rain. "I hear tires. Is that— I can hear them over the rain," he mumbles, staring into space, awe and confusion tangled in his expression.

Harper strains his ears, and sure enough, a car door shuts, and he can hear two sets of feet coming up the walk. He opens the door before Mayhem knocks, Manu standing behind her with a big clear umbrella held above their heads.

"Hey, that's my car!" Nova shouts, squeezing into the doorframe beside Harper.

"We thought it might be," Mayhem says, tossing Nova the keys. "It smells like Maya was in it—very recently."

But Harper is staring at the pickup, washers beating a lazy rhythm across the glass. He can't see his uncles, but he can smell them, even through the downpour.

"What do they want?" he growls, glaring at the driver's side.

Manu steps up to the door. "They came to talk to you. Your uncles, your aunt, and the elders." Harper opens his mouth, and Manu puts a hand on his chest, shaking his head. "You've wanted to know the truth, right? So stay calm and don't bite anyone's head off. They aren't coming in unless they can trust you aren't gonna freak out, and I want to hear what they have to say, too, so don't be a butthead. You can kick your feet all you want after."

Mayhem glances at him, trying not to smile, but Manu ignores her, trying to catch and hold Harper's eyes.

"What happened to your parents—it's not just about you, especially now. You get that, right? So can you be cool?"

He shuts his mouth, fire ants swarming under his skin. He wants nothing more than to shove Manu and Mayhem off of his porch and slam the door on them. But Nova's hand touches his elbow, warm and a little rough. He doesn't say a word, but Harper knows what he means, and he nods.

"I'm cool. I'm—" He looks down, sighing hard. "Tell them it's fine. Mason, let's try to make some space."

He steps from the door, and Manu and Mayhem move away, too, hurrying back to the cars. Mason wobbles to his feet and starts pushing the couch against the wall, the dogs licking his face all the while. But Nova stays where he is, gazing at his car keys with a wistful expression. His hand closes around the ring, knuckles paling. Harper watches him silently, willing him to stay.

Just a little longer, then you can run if you have to. Please just stay for now...

Nova looks up at him, his eyes green in the rain—large and uncertain. He swallows and hesitantly pockets the keys, joining Mason and the dogs. Harper stays in the doorway, watching as his family and the Libra elders climb out of their cars and scurry towards the house. He glowers as his uncles pass through, but says nothing—watching the room fill past its capacity: Aiden sitting between Uncle Heath's knees, Aunt Jelly at his hip; Oren's grandmother, Ambrosia Fisher, taking the armchair with Lila Magid standing at her side; and Manu and Mayhem and Mason and Nova all just trying to find whatever space they can on the floor around the dogs. Harper shuts the door, coming over to loom beside the couch, but not sitting by Aunt Jelly. She looks away, and he almost crumbles, almost sits down, but he promised to be cool, not to be cozy.

Not until he hears it all.

"You brats," Ambrosia says, her gnarled hands curling over her belly. She chuckles breathlessly. "I remember you, barely as tall as my knee, running all over my house and stealing cookies." She has aged, Harper thinks—progressed by 40 years instead of 20. How long has it been since he last saw her? His stomach aches, and he tries not to remember the smell of fresh-baked cookies, the sweet-cream aroma of her perfume hanging on the lace curtains, Oren's laughter muffled by fat cushions and fluffy rugs, and nothing more to worry about than getting caught with a handful of chocolate chips.

He maneuvers himself onto the floor between Mason and Mayhem. Nova has tucked himself into the furthest corner, the wall at his back. Harper tilts his head, frowning, but Nova avoids his gaze. Swallowing another sigh, he gives his attention to the Libra matriarch.

"There's still a little of that boy in your face, Harper Lovell. I see him even now. But I guess...more than anyone, I know why he's faded." She sighs, and Lila tugs nervously at her thick, black curls—hopelessly frizzy and gleaming with rain water. Aunt Jelly watches them both with narrowed eyes, and Harper wonders if Manu also had to knock on their doors—make them swear to a truce—before bringing them over. He wonders what kind of compromises were made. Or did they think that he, at nearly 25, was finally old enough to learn that his father had been alive all along and working with the enemy? He rubs eyes.

"Are you listening to me? I'm not saying this more than once. There's no time."

He drops his hands and sits up, makes his face polite and neutral. "Sorry. I'm listening."

"All of this began before your parents died. Maddox Hirst used to be a good man—that was the man you knew growing up, Harper. Five years before he killed Winter Lovell, he lost his son. His wife was inside putting away groceries, and the boy ran outside to check the mail. She didn't even realize he'd gone. A car hit him, and that was that. Maddox blamed her, and she left him—left town entirely. He never got over it. He started asking me and Lila about magic. Back then, we thought teaching him a little healing magic might give him a purpose, so we taught him the basics. We didn't know he was advancing his education outside our lessons.

"The year before your mother died, he went out of town for a time, and I'm guessing that's when he started building that pack. He began learning magic that no one should mess with. But that magic was just the means to an end he never should've reached for. The real problem was that he couldn't let go of his boy. He let his grief fester inside him until he couldn't see the lines he was crossing. He said he would do anything, as long as it meant his son was alive and safe again."

"But why start a new pack? Why not try to convince us to help?" Mayhem asks, twisting her braids through her fingers.

"Oh, he tried to convince us it was possible to resurrect his son without repercussions, but the only ones he managed to persuade were people who had also lost something—people who were desperate to save their loved ones, who were willing to let grief blind them to the consequences. It wasn't that I couldn't understand him, but I couldn't suspend my disbelief. I still don't believe they can bring anyone back without something horrible happening. I thought he'd give up, and if he didn't, he was so far down that rabbit hole, he'd end up killing himself in the trying—and that would be its own end. I never imagined he'd get this far. Who could have?"

"I could have," Uncle Heath growls. Aiden's hand goes to his shoulder, pressing him down against the upward impetus of his words.

"No, you could not have," Ambrosia bites back, rubbing her brow and looking even wearier, like she's repeating it for the thousandth time. "You weren't thinking about that at all. You just wanted revenge."

"I knew he'd cause more problems. I knew he was dangerous. *I knew we should hunt him down and get rid of him!*"

"And maybe we should have, Heath. Maybe we should have. But we didn't, because he was still pack."

"He was *not* pack. Pack is family, and family doesn't murder family."

"Why do you say he's gotten 'this far'?" Mason cuts in, softly and carefully. "What does 'this far' mean?"

Ambrosia turns, leaning forward and pinning her gaze on Mason. He fidgets, leaning into Harper unconsciously, and Harper stiffens, not sure if he's supposed to move away or not. There isn't a lot of space to move to. He looks away, trying not to smell the sweat and beer and sweetly citric hint of aftershave coming off of Mason with all that anxiety.

"Harper hasn't told you much, I'll bet, and we don't have time for a full lesson, so you'll have to get on with the condensed version. You know how in fairy tales, there's always a certain old woman you shouldn't insult? The one who everyone says will turn you into a mouse or a crow for stealing her vegetables? It turns out there's a pinch of truth to that. Long ago, a witch cursed a man who wronged her, and so we—"

"*The Witch!*" Nova lurches to his feet, looking around the room wildly. "Fuck. Fuck, fuck, fuck*fuck*."

He lurches towards the couch, eyeing the window with a feral, reckless expression, as though he's thinking of going through it. Harper jumps up, grabbing Nova by the elbow to get between him and all that potentially sharp, gutting glass.

"What? What's wrong?" Mason squeaks.

"That's what it was!" Nova's eyes move rapidly around the room, searching for an escape route. Harper tightens his grip, feeling his pulse beating against his fingertips. "That's what Lucía was trying to warn me about—the Witch! *Fuck!*"

"Nova—" Harper starts. "Nova, *calm down*. What are you talking about?"

"Shit, she's so close..."

"Who?"

"The Witch and Lucía and Fido— Fuck! *Fuck!*"

"Just stay calm. They can't touch you here."

Nova stares up at him, green folding on bronze folding on the tiny pricks of black at the center of his eyes—distant and unpredictable and ferocious, too. His arm remains taut, his body ready to run, but he doesn't bolt. He stills, turning his attention to the window and staring at the rain with an unpleasant, fixed expression.

"What does the Witch have to do with my parents?" Harper asks Ambrosia, carefully releasing Nova's arm. "What is Hirst trying to do?"

Ambrosia watches Nova, her brow splintering into a hundred fine lines. Her eyes never leave him. "Hirst wanted your parents in his new pack, but they were also against doing anything that unnatural and dangerous. It culminated in the fight that took your mother's life. I can only guess that he went in with the alpha magic already activated. He meant to convince them as friends, or dominate them as a wolf. He wanted them both, but the plan went south, and he made a run for it. Your father chased after him, and he wound up a beta. We didn't want to believe one of ours could do something so evil..."

"So you let him escape," Heath snaps, but he's cut off as Harper turns to face him.

"And you knew—you knew all along that Dad was alive. So what was that fucking funeral? Why let me think he was gone? Why didn't you tell me the truth? *Were* you ever going to tell me?"

Uncle Heath grimaces, and Aiden stares down at his knees, but Aunt Jelly gets to her feet, standing before him—four inches shorter but twice as tough.

"No, we *weren't* going to tell you. He bit you, too, Harper, and we'd already seen what that bite did to a grown man—someone with a lot more self-control and a lot more experi-

ence being a wolf. Bryce couldn't break free. Do you understand what that means? We didn't want him to get his hands
on you, too. Libra wouldn't help us deal with Hirst while
the trail was hot, so the only thing we could do was keep
you from going after him. So no, we didn't tell you, and we
weren't going to." They stare at each other, rigid and angry.
But then her face softens, and her eyes fall. She clutches
her elbow and slowly sits. "We thought we'd have more time.
Hirst was finally back in town, and for the first time in years,
we were so close. But then Maya..." She shakes her head.
"You're under the alpha curse. You and your dad. If either
of you is anywhere near Hirst, you won't be able to help it:
you'll turn on us. So you have to trust us to help you. You
have to trust us to do this without you."

"You've been hiding this fuckery for over a decade. You've
been lying to me since—"

"*Harper!*" Nova seizes on his shoulders. "Stop it! Maya's
in danger and so is Lucía, and they don't even know it! We
have to help them! We have to *go!*"

"What are you talking about? How do you know that?" he
asks, trying to pry free.

"Because the Witch has Lucía—she has Maya's girlfriend.
Hirst has been trying to force Maya to lead him to Lucía. He
wants the Witch."

"Exactly," Ambrosia interjects. "He wants to use her power
to bring his son back."

Nova nods, too close, too intense. "Before I came to,
Lucía and Hirst were in my dream, which means that Lucía
and the Witch are close to the lodge. If Maya dropped off
my car there..."

Harper starts, propelled back and forth as Nova begins to shake him.

"We have to go *now*."

"Their scent has probably been washed away." Harper glances at the rain-smeared window. "We won't be able to—"

Nova shoves him, and Harper trips over Manu's knees, barely managing to stay on his feet. "Are you really going to abandon her?"

"No," Aunt Jelly interrupts, "Harper *should* stay. Especially if Hirst does find them..." She reaches for him. He looks between her outstretched hand and Nova's angry eyes.

"I think she's right," Mason murmurs, "Maya can take care of herself. She has so far." He hovers beside Nova, hands firmly in his pockets, knuckles flexing against the fabric, unable to pull them out, to make that next move to stop Nova—not when Nova is like this, blistering and resolute. And Nova will go whether he's alone or not. He doesn't need them. Mason is right—together, Nova and Maya can do anything. They *don't* need him. They've never needed him, and if Hirst makes Harper attack Nova...

But even if Maya hates him, how can he just sit here, waiting for someone else to save her? If he deserts her now, what does that say about him?

"I have to go. She'd be there if it was me," Harper manages. His tongue is heavy and numb, stumbling over the consonants—his tone unclear and unconvincing. He searches for a space in the room devoid of eyes and finds none. He looks down at the floor, wanting to shrink, to become invisible, to hide in his loft until all of these people and all of these problems are gone. Nova stares at him, eyes hard. Mason watches him quietly, worried but sympathetic—and he wants that sympathy. He wants to be miles away, to never have become embroiled in any of this in the first place.

He wants a break.

"Are you sure?" Mason asks. "Are you *sure* she'd come back for you if the situation was reversed?"

"*She already did!*" Nova roars, but Mason shakes his head.

"I'm not asking you, Nova. I'm asking *Harper*."

"I don't know," Harper whispers, staring at Aunt Jelly's hand. "Maybe. Maybe not." Why are they all staring at him? Why does he have to make this decision with every face in the room judging him? No matter what he picks, there will be consequences. Big, heavy negative consequences. He presses his palms to his eyes. "I don't know! She doesn't— I don't think she wants my help. If I'm there, she might end up in even more danger."

"Then stay." Nova shakes his head and takes a step back, turning to push past Mason. He's never looked at Harper like that, never used that cold, final tone—like Harper is just another asshole on a long list of disappointments. And he's right. Harper knows he's being cowardly, clinging to excuses. In his heart of hearts, it's clear. The consequences probably will be terrible for him and Nova and Maya, but he knows what he *wants* to do. They left him before, but maybe that's because he made himself easy to leave—because he couldn't admit how much he cared, *because* he was the kind of person who could watch them walk away. He can't be like that anymore. He can't let them disappear from his life—not that easily, never again. He takes a shuddering breath, steeling himself.

"Wait," he says, stepping away from Aunt Jelly. "*Wait.*" And Nova does. He doesn't turn back, but he stops. "I'm coming with you. I'm— I'm coming, too. "

"Harper—" Aunt Jelly shakes her head. Mason watches, tight-lipped and fidgety. But Nova smiles, and Harper takes another breath, nodding.

"This is a bad idea," Mason mumbles.

"We can't let him go alone. What was the point of—" Harper glances at Mason's injured shoulder. Mason's fingers trace his bandages, face screwing into something between fear and frustration. "I'm not letting them take him again. I won't let them have her either. Whatever happens happens."

He holds Mason's eyes. Anxiety squeezes beneath his skin, but he remains resolute, and Mason finally turns, watching Nova already scrambling to the door, and closes his eyes, letting out a soft, defeated sigh. Harper pushes past him, hurrying after Nova, and Mason trails behind them at a dogged, unhappy pace.

They follow Nova to the hatchback. The pit in Harper's stomach expands and folds in on itself, growing deeper and denser with every footstep. It feels like the car is ten miles away, like he's running in a nightmare. Rain pelts the hood. The dogs tangle around their ankles. Someone is shouting for him to stop, but the sound fades into the downpour, becomes one more dissonant note in a deafening chorus, and he opens the back door and slides inside. But Nova doesn't put on his seatbelt or turn over the engine and peel out. He sits there, his hands clenched in his lap, and Harper wonders if he's having second thoughts (maybe the rain *has* washed away Maya's scent, what if Hirst makes Harper attack him again, what if Mason ends up turning on him, too?—reasonable, Harper thinks; they should all be scared as hell). His reflection disappears into the sheets of water rippling down the window, leaving Harper and Mason alone with the weight of his silence.

"What's wrong?" Mason asks, clicking his belt in and out of the lock, sounding a little too hopeful.

"Nothing. It's nothing. All that matters is getting to Maya before Hirst does." Nova looks up, his face working, trying to disguise the anxiety flooding his expression.

"Yeah." Harper swallows, looking through the rain towards the people emerging from his house, starting towards the car. "We better go if we're going."

Nova nods, unclenching his hands. "Just, if she's there... If the Witch really *is* there... Don't let her see me." He lowers his face, and in the rearview, Harper can see desperation in his eyes. But then Nova starts the car, and they're speeding into the driving rain.

ix. jude

*(rust like old bones,
under your nails, in your shadow
when you're alone)*

The porch has been breeding splinters all summer. Jude digs them out of her toes, her heel, the balls of her feet... The air feels hot, feels rough—too many cicadas singing all at once, too many crows cackling in the field. It chafes her skin, tugs her hair, annoys her.

She flicks a splinter into the seeding grass.

"Kya, kya," she mutters.

Poppa is angry again. Ever since Momma died, these fits come suddenly—springs of magma welling over his weathered face, flooding the empty halls and the creaking stairs, straining the bedroom windows... He is all the wasps caught between the glass and the screen, and his buzzing exhausts them all.

"You'll spoil her. You'll make her as strange as you."

"You neglect her. I'm teaching her important things."

"You're teaching her nonsense."

The door screams open, and he storms down the steps—

not a glance, not a word, cast her way. She crouches at the top of the steps and frowns, because Poppa has left dirty footprints all over her list, and she hasn't finished memorizing it.

Mamaw also comes out onto the porch, heavy around the middle and stiff in the spine. She settles into a rocking chair and sips her tonic water, squinting into the orange burn of afternoon over the field. They listen, both silent, as Poppa's engine turns over, his wheels whirring against gravel—at last finding purchase to jettison him down the drive.

They breathe a collective sigh.

"I hope it was worth it," Mamaw says, but she doesn't mean it the way other grandmas do. There's judgment in those words, a warning that Jude had better have learned something and not just horsed around all morning.

She throws herself onto her back, twisting her hair over her shoulder and pressing the blonde rope to her throat until her pulse jumps against her fingers. In two years, she will be 12, and old enough for the bite. She can't neglect her lessons. She can't give Mamaw a reason to hold that prize beyond her reach. She's hungry for moonbright paths, for the roll of muscle under thick fur, and the stretch of legs through rows of wheat and corn...

"These are the five things every wolf can do." She kicks, dislodging a mosquito from her ankle. "First, pack can heal pack. If it's a break or a scrape, the pack's tongue can heal it."

"But?"

"But..." She squeezes her eyes shut. "...you can't heal yourself, and you can't fix anyone who isn't pack."

"Good. Next."

"Wolves can visit the dreams of other wolves, as long as they're close enough. Mamaw, will you visit my dreams when I'm a wolf?"

"We'll have adventures you can't imagine."

"Is dreaming better than being awake?" She opens her eyes, staring upside down at Mamaw's slippers.

Mamaw breathes starlight into her glass. "For some. Not for us." Her breath whirls and glistens between the bubbles, rises to the surface and turns into icy flowers before melting away again. She gives Jude a conspiratorial wink, and Jude sits up, clapping for more, but Mamaw just tells her, "Continue."

"A powerful wolf can turn up to three days before a Moon, but on the night of the Moon, they'll become one whether they want to or not, and when the full moon sets, they'll return to being human again...whether they want to or not."

"Last two."

Jude frowns. She can't remember the last two. She leans on her knees, trying to peek at the steps without getting caught, but the writing makes no sense. It's gone all jagged colors and messy shapes—the kind of nonsense little kids make with their stubby fingers and clumsy wrists. She screws her brow.

"No cheating, Jude."

"But—" She leans forward.

Brown hands cover one step, brown knees obscure the next, and Jude narrows her eyes. "No fair."

"We all have to learn someday," Maya says—herself, but smaller. A shrink-ray Maya. Not a child, not like Jude.

Jude lifts her palms, stares into the crayon-stained creases, and she thinks: *Yes, this is true—I am like a child next to Maya.*

This is only one in a host of ways they differ, but it's the most important one, because Maya is better formed, more complete—greater. She is unafraid of life and of death. She takes risks that Jude cannot fathom. She is capable of the impossible. She went back for the hazel-eyed wolf knowing it could spell the end for her and Lucía—and for Jude, too—and Jude still can't wrap her head around that. It was supposed to have been obvious: save the girl, sacrifice the boy. If he managed to save himself, he would earn his place in the world. If not, it wasn't their problem. And so Maya's decision to avoid him—to avoid anything that might prevent her from reuniting with her long, lost love—was supposed to have been unambiguous.

But Maya had heard his cries, and she ran straight to him.

Does that mean that Maya loves her little wolf as much as she loves Lucía? Because until now, Jude was certain that Maya's love for Lucía was absolute and unwavering, and Jude would think a person only had so much room in their hearts (and their heads) for that kind of devotion. It should be incapacitating to care that much about two people at once.

She lowers her hands, ashamed of their stubbiness, the crayon and the dirt. She doesn't want Mamaw to notice. She doesn't want her to see how small Jude is compared to Maya. She might pick Maya over Jude, because Mamaw is like Jude: she can only care about one person at a time, and right now, that's Jude, but that doesn't mean it will always be her. This love might not last forever.

Because she dies.

She shudders and hugs herself tightly beneath the long, cold shadow that passes over the porch. "You won't die. You can't leave me," she whispers, peeking at Mamaw, but Mamaw only watches her with milky eyes and a stern frown, still waiting for her to finish the list.

"Did you forget?" Maya asks. She grabs Jude by the wrists. Her hands are deft and capable—quick to learn, and expert in their attentions; hard when they must be, but soothing in between. Jude's hands, trapped above them, look milky and frail, like the skeins of tissue that bind muscle to bone. They are unraveling, or they are forming. But they are not strong or steady or good. Jude is not good; she is not *enough*, and it scares her that Mamaw might look over and realize.

She tries to pull free, but Maya's thumbs trace Jude's arteries to her palms, and she shivers, trying not to breathe or close her eyes or feel. She doesn't understand why Maya has this effect on her, only that Maya's touch leaves her blistering and eager everywhere she doesn't want to feel anything at all. She grinds her knees together and scowls at a grasshopper preening on the edge of the step.

"A balanced pack engenders harmony. Even the boring old humans nearby experience it," she mumbles. "A balanced pack is a quiet forest; a balanced pack is a friendly town."

Jude wrests her hands, but Maya's thumbs dig into her bones. She writhes, relieved to feel pain where their bodies meet. She forces Maya, makes her fingers cruel, and she exorcizes the prickling-hot want from her skin.

She is too weak to also be vulnerable.

If it was me, would you do it?

Would you go back for me?

She rips her hands free, storming into the yard. Black-birds whirl around her. Their feathers gather on the path, black snow in the summer sun. She digs her toes into their oily fibers, breathing until her body is her own, and her mind belongs to itself and not the little voice in her chest.

"Are you angry?" Maya asks. "You didn't finish the question."

She squeezes her hands to her sides, presses her feet into the carpet of feathers. She wants to be a bird, wants to fly away and forget about Maya and Mamaw and everything else about being human.

She has become flustered, and she cannot let them know.

She measures her voice with care: "An angry wolf leaves rage in its wake. A scared wolf leaves fear. But only someone who truly knows another wolf's heart can feel its imprint on the world."

"Four out of five," Mamaw says. Her body clicks and groans as she shuffles to the edge of the porch. "How much time do you think I have?"

Jude flinches.

"Four out of five," Maya agrees. "You'll never outrun your bones like this."

Maya reaches for Jude again, and Jude lets out a frustrated screech, slapping her hands away. She turns and flees into the wheat. Her palms crush her ears, desperate to drown out their laughter, but the crows join in—all of them, *all of them*, jeering at her weakness.

If she could run fast enough, she would leave her skin behind.

And she would not go back for Maya.

She *wouldn't*.

She is too smart to make *that* mistake.

She breaks through the trees, where the black starts, and the sight stirs lucidity. Jude escapes into the dark, out of her own dream and into a cluster of pines. They don't smell like Jersey pines—this is something closer to home. She breathes, and her lungs swell with the afternote of a hot August ebbing into a warm, orange September. Desiccated leaves crunch underfoot, and the decaying scent of wilting honey-suckle gathers on her skin.

As she walks, the air grows cooler (though never *cold*). The leaves smell less like sunlight and more like loam. The oaks and maples turn barren, browned leaves gathering at their roots. She can hear hounds in the distance and the grumble of four-wheelers. She looks for crows, but the trees are quiet. Her nose twitches. There's a different kind of uncomfortable creeping into her pores. This dream is long, the dreamer's imagination more vast than a regular wolf's. She peers through the trees, but can't see anything, can't feel anything—no surrounding presence, no imaginary animals, nothing at all.

She looks over her shoulder, and she can no longer see the void. The edge must have moved back, because if it didn't, then this dream is so deep, she'll have a hard time getting out again. She kicks a nearby stump, rejecting the thought, and then she breaks into a run. She bounds over bushes and under branches, heading for the heart of the dream. She runs until the trees begin to thin, and then she skips to a stop, ducking behind a fat, black elm.

There's a single-wide trailer in the clearing just beyond.

The trailer has been painted white, likely with spray paint, because a rancid mustard peeks out where the white is chipping away. Rust seeps from the base of each window, creeping like sick down the sides of the trailer. Someone has built a wooden porch, but it sags in the center, befouled with patches of mosquito-rich water. The surrounding yard is just as miserable: rusting soda cans and shards of discolored glass glinting from the dirt; piles of rotting tires, coming apart at the tread, walling the treeline; an abandoned vegetable garden forever imprisoned behind drooping chicken wire—

The front door bangs shut, and Jude sees a blonde head pass through the front windows towards the checkered kitchen curtains. With nothing but aluminum walls to hold their voices, sound carries—becomes too big and loud for comfort. She feels a secondhand humiliation for the people inside, for their histrionics and their lack of awareness. Mamaw looked down on people like this, called them trash—no better than the debris littering the yard.

"You were supposed to walk home with her, Annie. Where is your sister?"

"I don't know! She was talking to Michael again."

"I don't want her talking to that boy. I need you to keep an eye on her. You're her older sister. She's your responsibility."

There's no sound in dreams—not really—just the impression a heart creates, so when the tattooed woman appears beside her, there's no snap of twigs or branches, but there is a percussion that accompanies her arrival, and it thrums between them. Jude narrows her eyes, taking in the woman's stocky physique; her peeling, twice chapped lips; the bruised, hooded eyes; and her dark, bobbed hair. Her tattoos have dissolved into dream water, nothing but red squiggles and blue smears bruising her skin. She reminds Jude of a character from a silent film—the woman who doesn't get the man, the one who tries to strangle the ingenue, and ends up tied to the stake at the end...

"Hmm," she offers in greeting.

The Anathema woman cannot hurt her in a dream. She would have to be a witch even greater than Mamaw, and Jude hasn't met anyone who comes close (aside from herself).

"Dandelion, you are spying," the woman says, her mouth smoky, but no cigarette to be seen. Jude has not smelled cigarettes since Poppa, and she vaguely recalls something about clove, but her memories of clove skew more towards Mamaw and braided loaves of bread—magic folded into the dough—to be sliced and buttered at dinner (wishes), or buried in the backyard and forgotten (curses).

"Ogre, your voice thins my nerves," she replies, baring her teeth.

"You have an ugly smile," the woman says and crosses her arms. One hand hangs aloft, dangling a cigarette that isn't there. She lifts it to her lips and realizes her mistake. Her hand curls around her bicep, and she grimaces.

"What is your name, witch?" Jude's lips skew, her smile stretching violence between cheek and ear.

"What is yours?" The woman stares at her, her oily face dour and flat. "We are not born fools. We become them."

Jude's expression flattens. "As you say."

The argument continues inside the trailer, battering the

walls, cracking the windows... Something about boys hungry for trouble and girls who never make it home.

"It is a bad look, watching a stranger's memory. This is a private thing."

"And still it is," Jude replies. "I care as much as a squirrel might." She clambers up the elm, taking a seat on a low branch to punctuate her point. "Are you all so traumatized?" she asks, kicking her feet, boot laces snapping the air.

The dark woman frowns, the serpentine muscle in her forearm hardening over her stomach, but brute strength means nothing in a dream, and Jude smirks.

"You have not lost anyone?" the woman asks, her voice dull.

Jude's legs slow. Her cheek twitches. "Who hasn't?"

"You want what we want."

"The Antlers Witch."

"Yes, to return the one you have lost."

Laughter cracks from her tongue—a peal worthy of frightened wings and battered stalks of wheat. But this dream is so pale and sorry, and her voice, unheard by the dreamer, is lost between the gaunt trunks of shortleaf pines—her audacity and her derision sadly muted.

"The dead cannot return. Death is a disease. Once caught, you cannot un-catch it. There is no cure, only prevention."

"I do not think this is so. If She can make little wolfies, why can She not also return life to the dead? In magic, hope is a necessity."

"No. Once we are in the ground, we belong to worms and rot and nothing else. Life concerns only the living. It's

ADDISON LANE

one of the oldest rules of the universe. You can prevent the future, but you cannot change the past."

"Then what do you need Her power for? Your companion? Is she sick?"

Jude tilts her head.

"Your sister's gone—gone when you were supposed to be taking care of her. This is all your fault, you lazy pissant!"

"Mom, stop! I didn't know!"

Glass breaks inside the trailer. Lots of things seem to be breaking, Jude thinks, noting fissures forming overhead. The walls of the trailer dent, struck by invisible fists, and the plexiglass windows pop free of their frames. Bits of sky fall in fat, oily spatters. Jude wipes a drop from her cheek, wrinkling her nose.

"Why do you think she is sick?" she asks, tucking closer to the trunk. A large, wet hunk of slate blue spills over her knee, and she recoils, scrubbing it away.

Disgusting.

The dark woman draws the hood of her rain jacket over her head and tucks her hands inside the sleeves. "You wish to prevent death. Whose death will you prevent? Our purposes are different, but not entirely, yes? Stop running. Join us instead. We can all have what we want."

"I want the Witch for myself, and I have no intention of sharing," Jude replies, dropping from the tree.

"There is no reason you cannot have Her, and we cannot have what we want, too. With Her power, it is a simple thing for all wishes to be granted. Tell your friend to stop running. We will help you find the other girl—"

"*I don't want to find her!*" Jude screams, and she knows she should not have said it aloud, because the truth surrounds her, no longer jailed, but a jailor.

She never wants to find Lucía.

She wants Maya for herself.

There is nothing in the world so frightening as *Lucía*, for Lucía will take everything from her—everything that matters. And why? What has she done to deserve Maya's love? Jude has been the one beside Maya all this time—the one she leaned on, who helped her get this far...

Has this all been a mistake?

"You are troubled," the woman chuckles.

"Silence, hag." Jude rubs her face, afraid that her thoughts are coming across too clearly, afraid that—at last—she has been seen.

"If you want to get rid of this girl, we can perhaps help with that, too."

For a moment, she is unable to stop herself—she entertains the possibility. Were Lucía out of the picture, perhaps she could become the Witch and remain with Maya. Who is to say it would be impossible? They could enjoy each other's company as they do now, safe from the ugliness of the mortal world, walking hand in hand into eternity—

But Maya is too human not to die.

And it would never go that way besides. There are certain moral contracts that, however simplistic or rigid they may seem to Jude, nevertheless bind people. She may choose not to abide by common principles, but she understands well enough: if she harms Lucía, she will lose Maya forever. She has not heard the children's story where the queen kills the princess and lives happily ever after.

She shakes her head.

"She will take what you want," the woman presses.

"She won't," Jude says. Pieces of the sky soak into her hair, dripping from the ends and gathering on the leaves below.

"Perhaps, but you are taking a risk. Is this not careless?"

"I can't take Lucía from Maya."

But she can take Maya from me.

She frowns at the blue welling between her toes.

"You are a stupid goat. That is fine. We do not need you, little witch. We only need your friend." The dark woman leers, her lips pursed around a satisfied smile. "And now we have found her."

The dream falls away, and Jude blinks up at Maya's honey-brown eyes, sleep fuzzy on her tongue and sandy in her eyes. It takes a moment to make sense of the racket: the slam of a car door, shouts between the trees, and heavy feet pounding the earth, headed their way.

"Jude, are you listening? We have to move. They're coming."

She takes Maya's hand, scrambling to her feet. They tear out of the tent and into the downpour, grabbing everything they can. Maya tries to break down the tent, but the slippery rope defies her fingers, and the uprooted canvas billows, plastering to the bushes.

"Just leave it," Jude shouts. "They're too close!"

A man laughs behind them. They whirl around, and the bearded man is there at the edge of their camp. Jude takes a step back and hears the bushes rustle. The sad-eyed man emerges from the sheets of rain behind her, followed by the alpha.

The bearded man wipes water from his face and grins a crooked, yellowing grin.

"Oh darling, we're *here*."

ABOUT THE AUTHOR

Addison Lane is a writer of queer modern fantasy.
She lives in New Jersey with her wife and two cats.
The Light in Her Dreams is the second book of
the Blackpines series.

Made in the USA
Middletown, DE
07 October 2022